Readers love
ANDREW GREY

Half a Cowboy

"…every book captures my interest and gets my emotions going. I am in awe of the fact that he can write so many books and have each one better than the one before…"

—Paranormal Romance Guild

Bad to Be Good

"Grey has a plethora of passages that convey the essence of his characters and the storyline."

—Love Bytes

Paint by Number

"This story, like most of Andrew's books is sweet and full of feelings… If you've never read a book from Andrew Grey and even if you have, I highly recommend this one."

—Open Skye Book Reviews

By ANDREW GREY

Published by DREAMSPINNER PRESS
www.dreamspinnerpress.com

Published by Dreamspinner Press
www.dreamspinnerpress.com

NEW LEAF

ANDREW GREY

Published by

DREAMSPINNER PRESS

5032 Capital Circle SW, Suite 2, PMB# 279, Tallahassee, FL 32305-7886 USA
www.dreamspinnerpress.com

New Leaf
© 2021 Andrew Grey

Cover Art
© 2021 L.C. Chase
http://www.lcchase.com
Cover content is for illustrative purposes only and any person depicted on the cover is a
model.

Mass Market Paperback ISBN: 978-1-64405-906-7
Trade Paperback ISBN: 978-1-64405-905-0
Digital ISBN: 978-1-64405-904-3
Trade Paperback published September 2021
v. 1.0

Printed in the United States of America
∞
This paper meets the requirements of
ANSI/NISO Z39.48-1992 (Permanence of Paper).

For Karen and Martin. You mean the world to me. I love you both!

Chapter 1

"HOW DID it go?" Julio, his agent, asked as soon as he picked up the phone. "Was I right? I knew this was a fantastic chance for you." He was bright and cheerful as he went on and on.

Finally Dex Grippon couldn't take it any longer. "Would you stop?!"

"What?" Julio asked, affronted.

"It was for porn," Dex replied. "They wanted a handsome, built guy to play the lead in a porn flick. Apparently they decided there was more money in porn than in the crappy horror knockoffs they had been doing. So instead of scantily clad girls running from a monster with a chain saw, they have naked girls running from a monster, and when he catches them... boom-chicka-mow-mow." Dex rolled his eyes. He had never been more embarrassed in his life. "When I went in for the audition, a bare-chested woman walked up to me, licked her lips, then told me to sit down. When I did, she straddled my lap and proceeded to feel me up." Dex heard Julio trying not to laugh on the other end of the line.

"Did you go through with the audition?" he asked with a squeak. Dex just knew he was about to fall apart.

"First thing, I do not want to be in porn."

"Not man enough for it?" Julio was about to lose it completely.

Dex would have loved to reach through the phone and strangle him. "I'll have you know that I'm a god in that department. But Mr. Happy does not come out and play with boobs and hoo-has. Secondly, I do not want to have to explain to my mother that the part I have been telling her for months is just around the corner is in a movie entitled The Bare Witch Project."

That was it—Julio lost it completely. The laughter rang through the phone, followed by a loud thump, then more laughter and a squeak. "Sorry."

"You fell off your fucking chair, didn't you?" Dex demanded.

"Yes," Julio said, still laughing.

Dex couldn't help smiling a little. Even he had to admit the situation was funny. He'd be laughing too… if he hadn't used most of his gas money to get all the way out to the valley for that stupid audition. And what for? Nothing. Now he was going to be eating grocery-store ramen for the next two weeks just so he would be able to pay his rent and not have to put any more on his already stretched credit card. "Asshole. Why do I have anything to do with you?"

"Because I'm your best friend," he croaked.

Julio was a very successful agent and worked with some of Hollywood's glitterati. He had taken Dex on because they had been friends four years ago, before Julio got lucky and signed the latest Hollywood heartthrob from a community theater in Van Nuys.

"And a pain in the ass. I know I'm not high on your priority list, but you could at least help me."

"Sweetheart… babe… I am helping you. I thought this was real." He paused, and the phone shuffled. "Look, I have to take another call. I'll be in touch soon when I have something else. There's a director who wants Georgie for a feature film, and I'll work you into the deal. There will be some smaller parts that we can use you for, and it'll give you a chance to make an impression on the director. That's how a lot of people get started."

Dex sighed. He had been doing that sort of thing for years. Yeah, he needed to pay his dues, but it seemed like that was all he'd been doing. Surviving on ramen was fine when a guy was in his twenties and hungry for success. But when a man in his thirties was doing it, it only meant he was hungry… and that was really sad.

Maybe it was time to just give up. He had been hustling from audition to audition for years now, and nothing had happened. Dex still had his looks and got noticed, just not in the way he hoped—and never in a way that actually led to something. "Thanks." Before he got the chance to say anything else, Julio was gone, and Dex was holding a silent phone to his ear. He tossed it on the sofa and sank into his chair, only to jump out again when the spring grabbed his ass.

"Dammit!" he growled. His life definitely hadn't turned out the way he'd hoped. He lived in a crappy apartment he could cross in exactly four steps from bedroom to kitchen. He'd picked up his furniture at secondhand stores… and, okay, sometimes off the curb.

Mother Hubbard had nothing on his cupboards, where he had three packages of ramen, a container of salt, and a drawer of condiment packets he could suck down if he was really desperate. This was no way for a man of almost thirty-two to live.

Dex checked the time, then figured he might as well get ready for work. Maybe if he got there early, he could catch a few extra tables and make a little more in tips if someone had called in. At least he could eat a meal while he was there; that was something. He changed clothes and checked that he looked okay in the mirror. Then he left the apartment, descended the four flights of stairs to the sidewalk, and got into his car.

"Please, baby. Be good to me. I promise to put gas in you at the corner."

When he turned the key, the old engine came to life, and he pulled out of the lot and headed to the gas station, where the car rolled to a silent stop at a pump. At least something had gone right today. Dex pulled out his wallet and parted with his last five dollars for gas, then went on to work—where he barely made it on time, thanks to traffic. Finally, after clocking in, he greeted his first customers and got busy.

DEX STUMBLED home to his tiny apartment in a northern suburb of LA after midnight. It had been a decent night for tips and his belly was full, so at least his stomach wasn't going to hate him all night long. After getting out of his clothes, he collapsed face-first onto the bed and fell asleep before he stopped bouncing.

Almost immediately, or at least it seemed that way, the phone rang next to his head. Dex started awake, hoping it was Julio with another audition. "Hello?" He was already halfway to the bathroom before he realized that the person on the other end of the phone was crying. "I'm sorry… umm."

"Dexter, it's Jane…. You need to come home right away." Suddenly, he listened more attentively. "It's your mother…." She could barely speak, but Dex's stomach wrenched. Jane was one of those people who took everything as it came with the strength and stoicism worthy of a Hemingway character. She was his mother's life partner. Dexter's father had passed away ten years ago, and afterward his mother had decided that she was going to be true to herself. She met Jane a year later, and they had been together ever since. Dex had never been prouder or loved his mother more than when she decided that she was going to live life on her own terms, even if he and Jane didn't always see eye to eye at first.

"What's happened?" He struggled to speak. If Jane was this upset over the phone, it had to be bad.

"She had a stroke last night. We got her to the hospital and she's in the ICU, but you need to get here as fast as you can. Do you need help getting a flight?"

Dex tried to think if he had enough money available on his credit card to pay for one. Probably not, given the fact that this would be last-minute. "I don't know."

"I'll get you a ticket and email you the details. It will be the earliest flight I can get, so you should start packing. Okay?" She sounded as frazzled as Dex felt.

"Yes. How bad is it?"

Jane didn't answer right away. "Just get here as fast as you can." She ended the call.

Dex hurried into his bedroom, pulled the suitcase out from under his bed, and threw clothes into it. Jane called him half an hour later with his flight information. She also sent him an email. He had four hours until he was scheduled to leave, which meant he only had time to call work to explain what was going on, let his landlady know he was going to be away so she could get his mail, and then leave for the airport. He knew he'd spend the whole early-morning cross-country flight to Baltimore worrying and wondering. What if he didn't make it in time?

"JANE, I'M almost to Carlisle," Dex told her when he stopped at a gas station the following afternoon to use the bathroom and get his fifth cup of coffee. "I'll be there in less than half an hour." It was hard to get his head around the fact that he was back where he'd grown up, twenty miles west of Harrisburg, a town not too big, yet not too small. Something about the place made everyone feel like they were home. With its unique mix of places and people, it walked a fine line. The place was old—like historical markers denoting where George Washington once went to church kind of old. Yet it had Dickinson College to keep it young, though the college itself was nearly as old as the town. The old courthouse had Civil War damage in the stone, and a block away, trendy new brewpubs did a great business. Big-box stores plied their wares on the edge of town, while antique stores, a gallery, a restored movie palace and theater, and even a candy store still thrived downtown. Somehow Carlisle had managed to change just enough to keep up with the times, but still held on to its roots.

Dex pushed back the wave of homesickness and returned his attention to the task at hand.

"Okay, sweetie. I'll tell your mom. Come right to the hospital. We're on the third floor, in the ICU. Just tell the nurses who you are and they'll let you in." She sounded on the brink of tears, and Dex wiped his own eyes and pushed the rental car to go as fast as he dared, letting the familiar scenery speed past.

At the exit off Highway 81, he was grateful the light turned green at the right moment, allowing Dex to speed through and get to the hospital parking lot. Once there, he hurried inside, hoping he'd remembered to shut off the engine. After following the directions to the ICU, he stopped at the desk, and a nurse led him right back to his mother.

He entered the private room, where she lay on the bed, her eyes closed, with Jane holding her hand. Dex did his best to ignore the equipment around her and just focused on his mother, the one person who had always believed in him, no matter how stupid some of the things he'd done might have been. "She knows you're here," Jane said, gently transferring his mother's hand to his.

"Hi, Mom." She lightly moved her fingers. "It's me, Dex. I'm sorry it took so long to get here." He got another squeeze, but her eyes remained closed. "Are you going to open your eyes so I can see you?"

There was no response this time. Dex lifted his gaze to Jane, who was leaning against the wall near the door.

"You need to get better," he continued. "I'm home now, and you and I can do all those things you like. We can go to the park and chase the geese back into the water so they don't poop everywhere, or we can count how many ducklings there are this year." He smiled as she once again squeezed lightly. Dex swallowed hard and tried not to completely fall apart. His mom had always been so vibrant, so full of life. She and Jane had a small house in Carlisle, near Letort Creek, and every spring the geese would congregate on their yard and crap everywhere. It was a constant battle between his mom and those poop monsters. His mother did all the yard work, and she kept the gardens like a showplace. Well, except for the goosey land mines.

"Is there anything you want?" Dex asked, desperately trying to get her to react.

"Sweetheart, she's here and she can hear you. Just talk to her," Jane said softly, staying near the wall. Dex suspected she was using it to keep herself upright. "She can hear you."

So Dex talked shared his porn audition story. His mom might actually have squeezed his hand harder. Dex hoped she was laughing on the inside. He told her about work and the people he'd met, and then he let Jane take his place again. He was running out of steam and figured some coffee would do him good.

He hurried away and found a coffee machine, where he grabbed two cups.

When he returned to the room, Dex found Jane with her head down, his mother's hand in hers. The machines were silent.

It took a second before he realized his mother was no longer with them. Somehow he managed to set the cups down before collapsing in the seat. "I'm sorry, Mom," he said quietly.

Jane lifted her head. "No, sweetheart. She was holding on until you got here. Once she heard your voice, she could leave. It was the last thing she wanted." Jane settled his mom's hand on the bedding and stood to gather Dex into her arms. "I don't think she would have lasted as long as she had if she hadn't been waiting for you."

Dex nodded and held her. He was alone now. Not that he had needed his mom on an everyday basis for a long time, but he'd known she was there for him. "I'm glad I got here in time." He'd had a chance to say goodbye, and that was the best he could have hoped for. "Where do we go from here?"

"All the arrangements have been made. Your mom and I preplanned. I'll call the funeral home, and they'll take care of everything."

Dex nodded. Jane was always the queen of lists, planning, and making arrangements.

"We can say goodbye now, then go back to the house." She pulled away and patted his shoulder. "I'll give you a few minutes alone with her." She left the room, and Dex sat next to his mom.

He didn't know what to say. To Dex, his mom was already gone, so sitting there with her wasn't important. He sat quietly, and when Jane returned, he gave her a few minutes before they left the hospital.

"I rode here with the ambulance and I haven't been home, so...."

"I have a rental." Dex led Jane to the car and then drove them home.

As soon as they got into the house, Jane seemed to fold inward. Dex couldn't blame her. He was exhausted himself. "Go lie down. I'll make some tea."

"There's some stuff for sandwiches in there if you're hungry." She wandered away, and Dex got something to drink, made a quick sandwich, and lay down on the sofa. It was dark when he opened his eyes once again.

Jane came down the stairs and shuffled into the kitchen. The scent of coffee reached his nose, and Dex groaned as he got up. He padded into the kitchen and sat at the table. "I'm going to miss her." Yeah, he was stating the obvious.

"I know. Me too," Jane said quietly. Dex was aware that this was so much harder on Jane than it was for him. He'd heard the tragic stories of Jane's life before she'd met his mother. She sat at the table, tears running down her cheeks. Dex got up and hugged her. "She was...." Jane broke down in tears.

Dex didn't say that he knew. Jane didn't need his pandering, only his support. She had been good to his mom and good to him. "You and I didn't always get along, especially at the beginning, but you've become an important part of my life, as well as my mom's. We're family." He closed his eyes, and they grieved quietly together for the most important person in each of their worlds.

Eventually, after watching some television and an obscene amount of stress eating, they both went back to bed. There were things to be handled, and the days ahead would be difficult for both of them.

"Do WE need to take care of the store?" Dex asked the following morning before the parade of people began making their way through the house. Dex fully expected a steady stream of his mother's friends to stop by.

"That's what I wanted to talk to you about. Your mother left specific instructions that Hummingbird Books and the building that it's in were to go to you. That store was something she started with your dad and kept going all these years. She said it was her one legacy for you." Jane put down her mug of coffee, opened the drawer under the same avocado-green wall-mounted telephone that he'd grown up with, and handed him a set of keys.

"But Jane, you...."

"I have all I need here. And this was something very important to her. She loved the store and she loved you. I don't know if she ever talked about it, but your mom loved your father immensely. She wasn't one of those people who married because it was the expected thing." Jane smiled. "Your mom didn't give two hoots about that crap. She adored him, and she loved me just as deeply." She sighed. "We were both very lucky. But your mom told me that the store was your inheritance, from both her and your father."

Dex swallowed. "Mom owned the building?" He hadn't known that.

"Yes. Your mom and dad bought it, then started the business. They lived in the front apartment when they were first married, right up until you were born. Your mom made the business a success while your dad taught at Dickinson. They had a good life, which only got better when you came along." Jane sipped her coffee and took a deep breath. "Once you started walking, they decided to buy this house and make it a home." She set down the mug. "But I'm sure you know all this. I'm just going on."

"And after Dad passed, she found you." She deserved to just talk if she wanted to. She'd earned that right by making his mother happy.

Jane nodded. "And she gave me love and a home here, which she left to me." She looked around the room at the chicken wallpaper and then laughed. "Your mom was many things, but a decorator was definitely not one of them. I tried to tell her that picking a theme for a room did not involve the amalgamation of chickens and foxes. But your mom loved both, so here we are. I keep coming in here and expect bloody chicken carnage all over the walls."

"Will you change it?"

"Not on your life," she said, sniffing softly, then refocusing. "People will start dropping by soon enough. I called Kyle, the guy who helped your mom in the store, and he was going to put up a sign that the store would be closed for the next few days. Everyone in town will know as soon as the obituary runs."

"Maybe I'll go down there and take a look around later." Dex was interested in seeing the place again.

Jane nodded and Dex sat back down. "Are you sure you're okay with these arrangements?"

Dex hummed his agreement and sipped his coffee, trying to get himself up and going before the grief parade began, with its endless food, low talking, and conversations of how special his mother was. "Yes. I honestly thought that everything would go to you and that would be the end of it." Now Dex had to figure out what he was going to do with the bookstore. His life was back in LA. Maybe he could put it up for sale. Then again, he suspected that the store had survived all these years simply because of his mother's personality and determination. He could sell the building, and that might give him enough money so that he could eat for a while. But it seemed a shame to sell real estate to pay for food. Fortunately he didn't have to know all the answers right now.

"I'm going to go upstairs to shower and get ready for the day. You know where everything is, right? Make yourself at home."

"Thanks," he said gently.

Jane left him alone in the kitchen, and he took care of the dishes before stepping into the downstairs bathroom… which immediately transported him to Whoville. It seemed his mother had redecorated in that room as well, including lime-green walls, hats hanging everywhere, cutouts of Dr. Seuss characters, and, inexplicably, a Cat in the Hat toilet-paper holder. There were Thneed hand towels, and a Lorax painted on the wall in front of the toilet with a thought bubble instructed the occupant to Think of the Trees. Dex sat down, laughed until he cried, and then felt guilty for reaching for toilet paper to dab his eyes.

He finished his business and then flushed. When he got up to wash his hands, the Horton cutout on the back of the bathroom door filled the mirror around him. I can hear the Whos… and you washing your hands. The script was backward on the door so it could be read in the mirror.

Dex washed up but refused to use one of the towels his mom had kept for company, so he found one under the sink, dried his hands, and left the bathroom. He returned to the kitchen and his mother's "carnage could happen at any moment" wallpaper. Covering his eyes with his hand, he finally allowed himself to feel the enormity of his loss. How was he ever going to go on without her?

Chapter 2

DEX WAS a more than a little overwhelmed. The house had been the scene of a steady parade of people from his past, many of whom still saw him as a twelve-year-old and insisted on telling him stories of what he was like as a kid. Dex smiled and waited until each conversation switched to his mother. Their faces would sadden and then they'd each share a special story.

A woman tugged on his sleeve, and Dex turned. She was maybe a little over five feet, dressed impeccably, and severely hunched over. "Your mother made the last few years bearable for me." Her eyes were filled with pain, and Dex just knew that for her, living had become a struggle. "I'm so grateful to her in so many ways." She held on to her cane as though it were a lifeline in one hand, and patted his shoulder with the other. "I always remember you as being such a good boy."

Dex smiled. "Mrs. Harper, I used to mow your lawn for you." She had paid him well but didn't hesitate to give him hell if he missed something. She had been old then—he figured she had to be in her nineties now. Still, he could still see the remnants of the person she'd been. Dex never remembered her at any time not looking her best— she always wore bright clothes with perfect makeup, just like now.

"Yes, you did. And you helped me in my garden." She smiled. Those shrubs and flowers had been her pride and joy. "You should come see it."

"Have you been able to keep it up?"

She gently patted him on the shoulder. "I may be old, but I'm out there every day for maybe an hour. The irises are blooming, and the peonies are about to start." She smiled brightly. "And I understand that you are keeping the shop going."

Dex hadn't decided that at all, but he didn't want to correct her. He had a lot of decisions to make and wasn't sure he wanted to return here permanently. Then again, his acting career was going nowhere, and he had just inherited a business and a building with a place to live.

"That's so wonderful of you. I have a few books that I need, so I'll stop by in the next few days." He got another smile, and then Mrs. Harper slowly made her way to one of the chairs, leaving Dex perplexed.

The younger woman with Mrs. Harper smiled at him. At first Dex wondered if she might be interested in him. "Your mom was a total godsend for her. Aunt Matty is in pain most of the time, and what your mom did…." She swallowed and gave Dex a smile before going to talk with her aunt.

Dex was confused. He'd had at least three similar conversations with other people about how much his mother had helped them, and they'd all ended with the person saying how thrilled they were that he was taking over the store and that they would be in. What puzzled Dex was whenever he asked them which books they wanted so he could have them ready, they looked at him as though he was a little off. And maybe he was, for even considering coming home. Dex was starting to wonder.

AFTER HOURS of talking and listening, Dex was worn out, and the time change was getting to him. Fortunately, he found Jane.

"Go for a walk. This will go on until the funeral. Your mother was loved, but it's going to be overwhelming if you don't take a break." She smiled. "Take the keys to the store if you want."

Dex gratefully went out the back door and through the yard, weaving along the back alley to the store. Then, after unlocking the rear door, he let himself inside.

The familiar scent of dust, books, and his mother nearly sent him reeling. This he remembered. Dex closed the door and turned on the lights as he wandered through the small back room with its boxes and shelves. His mother didn't keep much back here. She never had. She'd always said that she couldn't sell what was back here, so she kept as much of her stock out front as possible. Dex perused the area, remembering the corner where she'd set up a table and chairs. He had sat there for hours doing his homework, coloring, crafts—all of it in his own corner of the store. Oh, the hours he'd spent in this space with his mom. She always came back to check on him, and if there was no one in the store, she'd read to him or they'd color together until the bell on the front door jangled. It got to the point that he hated that bell because it meant she'd have to go back to work.

He peeked into some of the boxes before stepping through the curtain and out behind the register. The lights were off, but the sun shone in through the front windows. Everything looked as though his mother would return at any moment to open up. The shelves were all in order, and even the notebook she kept on the counter behind the register sat in its usual spot, surrounded by the trinkets and bookmark display. Dex lifted the counter and lowered it again once he'd stepped out from behind it, then wandered the aisles, looking over the rack of children's books. His mother had read most of them to him at one point. Of course, there were newer ones as well, but he continued on, checking over the shelves.

More books were turned cover forward to fill the shelves than he remembered. When he was a kid, the store had always been packed. But now it seemed staged—behind the single titles, there was nothing. The inventory he remembered his mother carrying wasn't in the store. Maybe it was just the children's section?

He continued to the adult areas of the store. There he found only a few hardcover books, and of the titles she had, his mother only had two or three copies. Dex knew independent bookstores had been having a difficult time in the past years because of Amazon, but every time he had asked his mother how the store was, she had told him it was fine. Maybe things hadn't been as rosy as his mother projected.

A knock on the front door startled him. He went up front, turned the lock, and opened the door. "Can I help you? We're closed for the next few days."

"I'm sorry. I was just passing, and I always stop by when I'm downtown." The man lifted his gaze, and Dex was struck by the most intensely blue eyes he had ever seen.

"My mother passed away and…." Damn, it was hard just to say the words. "The store will be closed until after the funeral." He put his hand over his mouth, willing himself not to fall apart. He had been okay a few minutes ago, but the grief was suddenly too much to bear.

"I'm so sorry. She was a nice lady." He paused, lowering his gaze slightly, looking like he might leave. "You're Sarah's son? She talked a lot about you. She said you were going to be in the movies." He smiled.

Dex swallowed hard. His mind skipped to how hunkalicious this guy was, with his hair all askew and his wrinkled shirt open just enough to allow Dex to catch a glimpse of a smattering of brown chest hair.

"Yes. I'm Dex." It was nice that his mom had talked about him. Even if he hadn't had any real success in Hollywood, his mother had always been proud of him anyway, he thought, his heart hitching.

"I was a regular customer of your mom's. I try to support local businesses, and she'd order in the books I wanted. That way she got the business instead of the big online places." He smiled, and Dex nodded.

"Did she have an order for you?" He wondered where his mother might have put it if she had.

"No. There were a few books I wanted, though. Still, I can come back once you're open again…." He leaned closer. "You are opening again, aren't you?" The blue in his eyes grew darker. "This is the only place in town that would order books for me. At least, the ones I wanted." He looked up and down the street. "I've got a weakness for romance—the masculine kind."

"I see…."

He put his hand over his mouth. "Of course. Sarah told me she had a gay son." He cleared his throat. "I'm sorry. I'm Les. Les Gable." He shook his hand. "I'm sorry to keep you. I'll come back later." He paused. "I just want to tell you that your mom was the greatest. She cared so much about everyone. I'm going to miss her." Then he turned and, with a wave, hurried down the sidewalk.

Dex closed the door and locked it again. It seemed his mother had had an impact on a lot of people in town. She had always loved books and got a great deal of joy from reading, something she had passed on to Dex.

He walked through the store before returning to the back room. He found the safe where his mother always kept it, and searched his memory for the combination. She had told him what it was years ago, and luckily the numbers returned to him. He opened it and peered inside, where he found less than a hundred dollars, her starting bank for the day. He also pulled out the store accounts book. Then he closed the safe door and locked it again.

He wasn't sure what else he wanted to do, but he didn't want to go back to the house. The grief gathering was probably still going on, and he'd had enough. His mother was gone, and Dex needed to try to process the loss alone. He didn't need dozens of people talking about his mother for him to know her. His mom was here in this building—in each book, as well as in the way she'd painted each wall a different color because she thought it would be cheerful. The only problem was that she'd picked the brightest colors possible. Dex was afraid his eyes would start bleeding if he didn't do something about it soon. Especially that grass-green carpeting. "Mom, I love you, but your decorating was a nightmare," he said out loud, smiling. That was his mother. She loved what she loved, and to hell with what everyone else thought.

Dex set down the books and headed for the bathroom, gasping when he opened the door. Apparently where the bathroom in the house was Whoville, the one in the store was all Alice in Wonderland, and it had gotten the same treatment, including a Mad Hatter toilet-paper holder and a Queen of Hearts toilet cozy. The White Rabbit bounded over one of the walls, but it was Alice being sucked down the rabbit hole that made him laugh. It came with a reminder to flush. This was his mother in a nutshell. She could be out there, and yet she could also be so clever.

He shut the door, unable to use the bathroom, and retrieved the record book. It was time to go back to the house. At least now he could review his mom's records and figure out if it was viable to keep the store going.

He had a task to accomplish, something that would fill some hours and keep him from moping around. If the store was his mother's legacy, Dex needed to see if there was a way to move forward. He pulled open the rear door and locked it behind him, then headed back toward the house.

He decided to take a roundabout route, walking down to the square as the clock in the old courthouse chimed the hour. He paused and smiled. He remembered being in the store, listening for that bell, because most days, when it chimed six times, his mom would close up and they would go home. He shook his head as if to clear the memories. Something around every corner seemed to remind him of her. The trees had all leafed out, shading the streets. Dex wiped his eyes. In his mind's eye, he could see his mom and dad in their backyard, music drifting out from the house as they danced to a cascade of flower petals.

At the time, he'd considered it horribly embarrassing, especially when his mother had backed away from his dad insisting that she teach Dex to dance. Dex had fought it with everything he had. He hadn't wanted to learn to dance. But she'd made him. Damn, what he wouldn't give to dance with her with one last time.

"Dex?"

He turned and once again met Les's blue eyes. His heart beat a little faster and his throat dried in an instant, especially seeing the heat and interest in those eyes. Dex was used to people looking at him with hunger, but this was something more. "I just left the library and was on my way back to my apartment. What are you up to?"

"I finished up in the store and figured it was time to go home." He nodded in the direction he was going, and Les fell into step along with him, walking slowly. Dex realized that his one leg seemed stiff. He shortened his usual stride so Les wouldn't have to strain to keep up.

Les smiled at him. "Sarah always told me stories about you when I was in the store. She said that you're an actor working in LA."

"I haven't been working all that much lately, unfortunately. Unless you count porn," Dex said, his voice deadpan.

Les stopped midstride. "You did porn?"

Dex shook his head, grinning. "Oh God, no. My last audition was supposed to be a serious role, but well, it didn't turn out that way. My mother was always supportive, but I can't help but think her support would not stretch to cover that." He chuckled. "Though maybe Mom would have just told me to do my best, then rented a copy later so she could tell me what I'd done wrong." He chuckled. "I would have to say that the most embarrassing thing I can think of is my mother going out to get a copy of Shaving Ryan's Privates or something, so she could rate my performance."

Les chuckled. "It must have been nice to have that kind of support in your life. I never did. My family wasn't anywhere near as open-minded as your mom, that's for sure. My folks were very predictable. 'You will go to college, you will go to church, you will not be gay or have gay thoughts.'" The humor left his voice and his posture became more rigid when he spoke of his parents.

Dex had always known he'd been lucky, especially when it came to his mom, but he sometimes forgot how fortunate. "I never knew how Mom was going to take anything. You remember what it was like to be a teenager and all you wanted to do was shock your parents? I'd do that, and Mom would look at me and say, 'It's okay, I support you and will always love you.' Then the next day she'd decide that the upstairs bathroom needed painting and I'd walk in and get a surprise of my own when the walls were jet black... or neon yellow. The hall bathroom upstairs has been both at one time. I think it was her way of shocking me right back. And her offbeat decorating skills usually did the trick."

Les laughed out loud, his stance loosening. "She would do the funniest things. One time when I came into the store, she had the shelves pulled back from one of the walls and was painting it Barbie pink, just so she could see how it would look."

"That's my mom," Dex agreed.

"At least she liked color. My mother painted the entire house this off-white color. She called it Palest Peony or something, and every wall in every room was the same color, all through the house. I had to beg her to let me do my room in blue. She eventually let me, but only if I promised that if it didn't work out, I'd paint it back. The furniture was every shade of brown, and the carpet beige. It was like living in a forest in permanent winter. Mom's idea of adding color was bringing in black accents... because they went with everything." Les began to laugh. "My dad hated it. So for Christmas, he used to get her really bright knickknacks. They would be on display for a while and then suddenly they'd disappear." He smiled.

"You're kidding, right?" Dex asked. When Les shook his head, Dex added, "You should see the guest bedroom upstairs. It has this psychedelic wallpaper, as if the person who created it had done acid back in the sixties. I have no idea where Mom found it, but I'm surprised anyone who's stayed over hasn't suffered from seizures." He paused. "You know, that could be why Mom didn't get many guests. They'd stay one night and detour to the hospital on their way out of town."

Les shrugged, smiling. "You know what they say—after three days, both fish and guests begin to stink. Maybe it was her way of controlling the odor." He tilted his head adorably to the side, and Dex took a second to enjoy the view. Les had a strong jaw and an expressive face that pulled Dex in. His high cheekbones gave him an almost regal look, and yet his eyes danced with mischief. And he had a sense of humor, which was necessary… if just to get through the trials and tribulations of life. Dex had definitely needed one with his mother. She had sometimes been a handful.

"My mom's guest room…."

"Let me guess, slightly pinky off-white," Dex teased.

"Yup. I remember having a friend for a sleepover. I showed him into the room—he set down his bag and fell onto the bed, asleep instantly." He grinned and Dex rolled his eyes before chuckling lightly.

"So your mom was color-challenged. And mine was a color ninja, never afraid of anything." They approached the house, and Dex groaned as a couple went inside carrying a casserole dish. "I swear to God, the house is going to explode with all the grief food people are bringing." He patted his stomach, which did a little roll at the thought. "Want to hazard a guess as to the number of pounds of macaroni and cans of soup that have given their lives already?"

Les shook his head vehemently. "Not on your life." He patted Dex's shoulder, and heat spread through him from the touch. "I need to get home too. But I'll see you later at the store?" His gaze met Dex's, and Dex nodded but made no effort to move away. There was something incredibly attractive about being lost in those eyes, and he was in no hurry to return to reality. Les licked his lips, and just like that, Dex wondered how he tasted. Les was a feast for the eyes, and his musky scent wafted on the breeze. Dex swallowed hard, wishing for more, but there were limits to what he'd do with a guy he'd just met.

It was bad enough that Dex had done things he could never tell his mother in order to try to secure a role. He suppressed a shiver thinking about it. This wasn't Hollywood. Les was just a handsome guy. "I should go inside and make sure Jane isn't overwhelmed."

Les nodded, and Dex shook his hand, then forced himself to turn away from him and walk inside the house, where the half-whispered conversations were almost overwhelming. Yelling he could understand. Even crying, for that matter. But a dozen whispered conversations, each one just soft enough that they were impossible to hear, created a low din that was annoying as hell.

He found Jane in the kitchen with two other ladies. "Take this into the dining room, please," Jane asked one of the ladies as she pulled a casserole dish out of the oven and set it on top of the stove.

"I can handle this," Dex told her softly.

Jane shook her head and leaned close. "If I have to sit in here talking about Sarah for another minute, the wallpaper chicken carnage will be from me." She removed another dish from the oven and started pulling some of the salads out of the refrigerator.

"You know if you feed them, they'll never go home."

"That's okay. This is what Sarah told me her family does. You might remember it from when you lost your dad. They gather and stay together until the funeral. It's just one of those things that they do to try to comfort each other."

Dex hadn't known that. Though now that he thought about it, he remembered times when his mother went to sit with his aunts and uncles and how they came to sit with them when his dad had died. That must have been her way of doing her duty without getting him involved in the whole grieving marathon. "They'll leave later this evening and then come back tomorrow to 'help' with anything."

To Dex, it looked like Jane was going to be "helped" into a nervous breakdown. "Come on. There are some things I want to talk to you about," Dex said loudly enough for the others to hear. "Let's go out in the yard." He hoped the rest of the family would have the sense to leave them alone.

Dex filled a couple of plates before heading out back. Jane followed, and they sat under the umbrella on the large patio.

"What did you need?" she asked as he slid a plate in front of her.

"Peace for a few minutes," he answered, and Jane's shoulders slumped as tension escaped her. "Just relax for little while." They both needed to breathe. The change in both their lives was monumental. Trying to take those first steps with a house full of relatives was exhausting.

"I have no idea why your Aunt Grace is even here. She and Sarah hated one another, and now she's acting like they were best friends." She took a few bites.

Dex got up, headed to the kitchen, opened the far lower cupboard, and pulled out a bottle of fine sipping whiskey.

"That isn't a good idea," Aunt Grace said as she wiped down the counter, hopefully getting ready to leave soon.

"Maybe not for you, but I damned well need one." He glared at her before grabbing two glasses and going back outside, leaving her disapproval in his wake.

"I thought we could both use one." It was his mother's favorite. Dex poured a dollop into each glass and handed one to Jane. "To...." Words failed him, and his throat clenched.

"The greatest broad that ever lived," Jane supplied, and Dex nodded. That was the best description of his mother he'd ever heard. She was over the top, joyful, loud, thoughtful, and always the life of the party. Dex clinked Jane's glass, and they both sipped before downing the rest of the smoky, rich liquid.

Dex set down his glass and poured a little more for each of them before screwing the cap on the bottle. "I met one of Mom's customers today—Les. He stopped by the store, and then I ran into him on the way home. He seemed really nice."

Jane nodded. "He's a good man. Your mom thought a lot of him. He's a little younger than you, I guess." She smiled and leaned over the table. "He came into the store maybe two years ago looking for something different to read. Sarah said he approached the counter and quietly asked if she sold gay romance. Sarah told me all about it when she got home that night. She helped him order a dozen different books, and he's been ordering from her ever since. But after that first time, your mom added a rainbow flag decal to the front door. She wanted people to know that her store was a safe place." She lowered her head, her shoulders rising and falling. "She had the biggest heart of anyone I've ever met."

"I know. Remember the never-ending parade of stray dogs and cats she was always taking in and trying to find homes for?"

Jane laughed, even as the tears ran down her face. "That damned yellow cat." They both grinned. His mother had found a raggedy yellow cat and taken him in. That cat loved her to death and hated everyone else. "Every damned time it came near me, it took a swipe at my legs. I had scratches for two fucking years."

"Yup. I had to get a tetanus shot once because of him." Dex covered his ear out of habit. That damned cat loved to attack from on high.

"He'd sit on your mother's lap and hiss at me when I came into the room," Jane added.

"But he's just misunderstood," Dex said, doing his best impression of his mother, and they both laughed again. "And let's not forget the pooping pup."

"Oh Lord. That dog refused to go outside. It pooped everywhere except on the grass. But your mom loved that walking fertilizer factory. She fought me until she learned he was really sick and had to put him down. Sarah cried for days until she found another stray." She reached for the bottle and poured herself a little more. "I was one of her strays."

That was news. "How? Mom loved you dearly."

"I know that. But after my marriage broke up, I was so lost. I never would have met your mom if it hadn't been for the store. I started reading a lot because I didn't know what to do with my time. Did you know she started her classics reading group because of me? She said I should read classic lit written by women, and after Jane Austen, the Brontës, and others, we became friends and it slowly deepened to more. She and I didn't have one of those grand love moments—it just built. And then she asked me to move in with her."

Dex sat back. "How come you never married? I always hoped you would. You and Mom always seemed so happy."

Jane's eyes widened. "She didn't think you would want her to, and she didn't want you to be unhappy." She took another sip of her whiskey. "I guess I assumed the two of you talked about it."

Dex shook his head. "I would have asked to stand up for her… hell, both of you. I always hoped you would just do it, but she and I never talked about it. Assumptions, I guess."

"Make an ass of u and me," Jane finished. Dex nodded, wishing he could go back and tell his mom what he thought. "Your mom and I had a good life together. I like to think we were good for each other, but you know your mother. She helped everyone, but she kept a lot of things to herself."

"Jane," Aunt Grace called from the back door. Their time was up. Jane stood, and Dex did the same. They probably should have counted themselves lucky they had been left alone this long.

Chapter 3

ANY OTHER day, Les would have been prowling around his small apartment—it was over one of the restaurants downtown and across the street from the bookstore he used to watch—but his foot hurt today. The bookstore was still closed, and he had read in the paper that Sarah's funeral was today. He thought of using his skills to let himself in the back door so he could look around. It wasn't likely that anyone would be there, and he'd have plenty of time to check the place out thoroughly and find out what Sarah had been up to. His cop senses told him something wasn't quite right, especially with the level of business she was doing. It shouldn't have been enough to keep the place in the black.

The only thing stopping him was the fact that he had really liked Sarah. She had been a kind person, and her drive to help him had been genuine. They were friends, in a way.

Les sighed and sat down in his old but comfortable chair.

Ever since he was a child, he had dreamed of being a police officer. His father had been one, but that wasn't why Les had wanted to join the force. It had been because of his uncle Mark. He'd taken Les in after things with his parents had gone to hell. Mark had always been larger than life—strong, powerful, calm, thoughtful, a great cop... heroic, even. And that was what Les had wanted to be.

He'd succeeded for a while, and was even working on a career-making drug case. But in the end, his dream of being a cop had cost him everything. Because of one takedown gone wrong, he now walked with a damned limp and had continued weakness in his foot and leg.

More than anything, he wanted to rejoin the force, to prove he could still do the job. And maybe if he figured out what Sarah had been doing to keep that store of hers afloat, he might get that chance. Because she was definitely doing something, and his cop instincts were screaming that it wasn't legal.

Sure, he'd be largely on desk duty because the leg wasn't going to allow for much more than that, but at least he'd prove he still had what it took.

He wasn't thrilled about scrutinizing the activities of someone he considered a friend, but it was a chance—maybe his last one—to get part of his life back. He'd been close to breaking a statewide drug investigation when he'd been injured and forced into medical leave.

That case was still open, and his instincts told him that Sarah and her store could somehow be involved. He hated himself for thinking that way about a friend, yet his suspicions wouldn't go away.

Les put his foot up on the coffee table and sighed as some of the pressure eased and the discomfort slipped away. He closed his eyes, and an image of Sarah's movie-star son flashed in his mind for the millionth time since he'd first talked to him. "Shit." Then he checked the time and stood, ignoring the renewed discomfort. He changed clothes and then left the apartment, heading for the large, historic church on the square.

When he arrived, Les sat in the back pew on the aisle. That way he could watch Dex as he came in and sat with Sarah's partner. Okay, he knew he was acting a little creepy, but Dex was the first guy to pay attention to him since his injury. Les had tried going to the clubs in nearby Harrisburg, but the guys there weren't interested in someone who could barely get around. They wanted someone who could dance all night and then take them home for more athletic activities.

The service began, and Les sat quietly, thinking of his friend who would no longer be there. He tried not to think about what Sarah had been up to. She was gone, and whatever she'd been doing had likely died along with her. No good could come of him continuing to watch the store and its customers for a possible link to the drug operation that should no longer be his concern. But it was hard to give up completely on something he'd worked so hard for. Besides, he liked Dex. Maybe it was time to let all of this go, including his obsession with getting back on the force.

Throughout the service, he ruminated on his own issues. Before his injury, he'd been a strong, tough police officer, confident that he was infallible. He'd chosen his small apartment because he was never home. It had been a place to eat and sleep, while he'd spent his hours out doing what he loved. But in one day, all that had changed. Now his tiny apartment was his refuge… and his prison.

Les got up to leave when the others did, pulling his thoughts back to the present. He filed out with everyone else and made his way along to the fellowship hall, where lunch was being served. He got a cup of coffee and took a seat at one of the tables off to the side.

He hadn't expected anyone to sit with him—they all seemed to have their groups—but Dex surprised him.

"Hi, Les." Dex sat down with a cup of coffee and a plate of fruit in his hand. "Thank you for coming. Mom would have appreciated it." He half smiled, his mouth drawn and dark patches under his eyes.

"Looks like you've had a rough few days," he said quietly.

"Yeah. At least after all this, the house will be quieter. But now we have to figure out how to have a life without Mom." He seemed a little lost.

"I kind of know what you mean. My parents are still alive, but I haven't spoken with them in quite a few years." He sighed and pushed away the old hurt. There was nothing he could do about his parents' attitude, and he wasn't going to go crawling back to them. If he hadn't after the accident, when they had said he could live with them as long as he didn't bring his "lifestyle" into their home, he wasn't going to now.

"I guess there are many ways to lose people," Dex commented quietly.

Les nodded. "You know, this is a funeral and all, but I'm willing to bet that this conversation is probably the most depressing one in the room." He smiled, and thankfully Dex did the same.

"God, yes. Mom would have hated this. She loved life." He sipped some coffee, and his incredibly big and expressive eyes took on energy and a touch of excitement.

"Then let's talk about something more fun. What's your favorite memory of your mom?" Les smiled. "She used to tell me all kinds of stories when I came into the store."

Dex chuckled. "Mom had a story for everything. One time I asked her about volcanoes, and she told me about the time she went to Hawaii and visited the volcanoes there. She described the rivers of lava and how they flowed toward the sea, where they cooled instantly and sent up clouds of steam that billowed up with the waves." He leaned forward.

"There was this picture of a koala on the wall of the store, and when I asked her about it, she told me about the time she got to hold one. She said it had long claws and it was like holding eucalyptus-scented steel wool." Les sipped his coffee. "She really made me want to go to Australia." When Dex laughed, he asked, "What?"

"Mom never went to Australia or Hawaii… at least not in real life. She was a reader, and almost all of her adventures were experienced through books. Of course, when I was a kid, I thought my mom's stories were the greatest things ever. She took me on pirate adventures and on expeditions through the jungles of India. She told me what it was like to travel on the Orient Express, and she described Paris to me, as well as all the museums there." His expression softened. "I used to tell Mom that when I made it big, I'd send her and Jane to all those places she told me about." He sighed loudly. "I never got to do that."

"She never traveled?" Les asked. It seemed weird that she told stories about places she'd never seen.

Dex shook his head. "Oh, in her mind she had, because she'd read about it. It took me a long time before I understood that Mom was the ultimate homebody. She wasn't interested in going anywhere. Instead, she lived vicariously through the stories she read, without having to pack for days, get bitten by bugs—big bugs—or worry about snakes or spiders. And when her glass of wine was empty, she could pause, open another bottle, then return to her adventure. I guess that's my favorite memory of her. She wanted me to have adventures, so she read and told me stories. I wouldn't be the man I am without them."

"Talking about Sarah and her stories?" Jane asked as she sat down with them. "She once told me about this trip someone took on a raft from Peru to Tahiti… or somewhere like that. I didn't know it was a voyage someone else made in the forties. Sarah was a great storyteller—she always made her tales seem so real. Then she'd make an amazing dinner, and we never had to leave the house." She put her head in her hands. "I'm going to miss those."

Dex took her hand. "Me too."

Les knew he had no right, but he felt a little jealous of Jane. He wanted Dex to take his hand like that. Not that there was anything logical to his reaction. Les had just met Dex a few days earlier, and they had only walked and talked a little.

"When I first met her, I didn't realize that her stories were just that. I thought she had traveled to all these exotic places, and when she told me the truth, I was angry with her at first. But that was just part of who Sarah was. She loved stories—reading them and telling them."

"And, apparently, decorating," Les interjected, which launched another round of tales about Sarah's adventures in paint and wallpaper.

"I swear"—Dex put his hand in the air—"when I moved to California, she sent me a box of wallpaper with palm trees and surfers on it because she saw it in a catalog and thought it would look wonderful in my LA apartment." He lowered his face. "I didn't have the heart to tell her that there was no way I'd ever use it. So I tacked a few rolls onto one of the walls, took a selfie in front of it, and then rolled the paper back up. The stuff is still in the back of my closet. I never had the heart to throw it out. Maybe someday I'll find a kid who will like it."

Jane chuckled. "She always thought of you as her baby. It didn't matter how old you got—you were still her only child. I think it's like that for all parents."

Les's throat began fill, and he reached for the pitcher of water in the center of the table and poured himself a glass. Unfortunately, he knew firsthand that Jane was wrong. His family was in the next town over, and yet he never saw them. "I wish I could say it was," he said softly, then wished he had kept his mouth shut. This was a funeral, and Dex and Jane were trying to deal with loss. They didn't need him unpacking his baggage. "What else did she do?"

"Sarah was an amazing cook," Jane supplied, wiping her eyes.

"Mom read all kinds of books, including cookbooks." Dex turned to Jane. "Remember when she got a used copy of Mastering the Art of French Cooking and decided that she was going to try her hand at making duck?" Dex laughed, and Jane fanned the air in front of her.

"We were lucky the fire department didn't show up because of all the smoke. Sarah didn't remove enough of the fat from the bird, and the danged oven nearly caught fire. There were flames shooting out the door when she opened it. I slammed it closed, turned it off, and opened all the windows in December. The house was freezing for hours. Thankfully the flames died quickly, but dinner was burned to a crisp."

"We had Chinese for Christmas dinner that year," Dex added with a grin.

Les put his hand over his mouth because he didn't want them to see him laughing. "You're kidding? Christmas dinner?" He could just see the smoke pouring out of the open windows and the holiday being ruined.

Dex nodded. "We had a great time. It was snowing, and Mom set fans in the windows to pull the smoke out. It took a while, but she cleaned up after the burnt offering that had been dinner and placed an order for Chinese. Jane went and got it."

"By the time I got back, the smoke still hung in the air, but everything else had been cleaned up and what was left of the poor duck was in the trash. Sarah could be a real ballbuster when she wanted something done." Jane turned to him. "You get that from her."

Les snickered as he shifted his gaze to Dex. "That's good to know." He winked, and Dex chuckled, not missing the double entendre.

"I think I need to circulate or something," Jane said, slowly getting up. She looked tired and her feet seemed leaden.

"Why don't you just sit back and relax a little? People can come to you," Les offered. "Do you need anything to eat or a refill on your coffee?" When she nodded, he got up, then brought back the coffee pot and a plate of dessert. Maybe something sweet would help raise her spirits. He set the plate down, then filled her cup. After he returned the coffee pot, he noticed that others were starting to join them at the table. It seems he had been right—they were coming to her.

Dex got up too, leaving one more place at the table, and stood near him. Les knew this wasn't the time, but he couldn't help himself. "Are you going to open the bookstore?" Les asked.

"I haven't decided," Dex answered as he drew closer. "It was Mom's dream and what she loved. I need to look over the accounts to figure out if the store could be viable long-term. Mom seemed to be able to make it work." He bit his lower lip. "I'm not even sure if I want to come back here to live. I have a home in LA and…." His words tapered off. "Heck, what am I saying. I have a few friends out there and a career that's going nowhere and isn't likely to." He scratched his head lightly. "I'm thirty-two, and there's a whole crop of youngsters with fresh faces and even fresher dreams looking to take Hollywood by storm. I'm almost over the hill—I'm never going to get those really good roles that I've always wanted so badly. And if I can't get them, what's the point?" Dex sighed. "Maybe opening the store and seeing if I can make a go of it is the best thing to do." He smiled. "The most interest I've had lately…."

Les grinned. "Was for the porn?"

Dex laughed as he nodded. "Yeah." Even though he smiled, Dex's eyes betrayed his disappointment. It was clear to Les that acting, and Hollywood, had been his dream. Les knew what the death knell of a dream felt like. But he wasn't going to go there.

"Let me say that I hope you decide to stay." He flashed his best smile and got one that was almost blinding in return. Dex really should be in the movies. His face was so expressive, and his eyes drew Les right in. Les's heart beat a little faster, and he had to remind himself that they were at Dex's mother's funeral lunch.

"I guess I have a number of things that I need to figure out," Dex said.

"If you need some help in the store…," Les offered. "Right now I'm off work because of my foot, and I could use something to fill some of the time." Why hadn't he thought of offering to help in the store before? He could get a chance to look around and spend some time with Dex. Hopefully he was all wrong and the hunch that there was more to the business at the store than met the eye was false. He hoped so, for Dex's sake.

"That would be nice," Dex said. "I have to go over the store's books, but if possible, I'd like to open before the weekend. And if I'm going to do that, I want to try to repaint. It could use some sprucing up, and those colors are going to make my eyes bleed if I have to be there all day. Maybe if I give the place a little facelift and make it more inviting, I can bring in a few more people."

Les supposed it was worth a try. The store had been Sarah's, and it was a reflection of her. Les was going to be sad that it changed, but if Dex was going to take it over, then he would have to make it his own. "I'm pretty good with a paintbrush."

Dex nodded and smiled. "I'd love the help, but I don't have the money to pay you, and it wouldn't be right to ask you to work for nothing. Maybe when the store is open and I have some business coming in...." He seemed overwhelmed.

"I'm not asking to be paid. Helping out people is just something I like to do." He hoped he didn't sound creepy.

"Then I'll probably pick up some paint tomorrow. I want to the place to be cheerful and bright, but not over the top."

"Maybe you could try a pale yellow," Dex offered. "It would seem kind of sunny, but not so bright that it was glaring."

"Good idea. I'll stop at Home Depot in the morning and grab some paint and supplies. Hopefully I can be to the store at nine." He grinned. "And I'd appreciate the help. I really would."

"I should be able to be there. I don't have anything going on tomorrow." He didn't want to admit that the only plans he had involved sitting at home in front of the television with his foot up, doing nothing. Maybe some activity would be good for him.

Jane left the table, and Dex followed her with his gaze. "Okay," he said softly. "Thanks."

A number of people looked like they were ready to leave, so Dex nodded to Les, then joined Jane by the door, where she was thanking their guests for coming. There was no reason for him to stay, so Les left as well. As soon as he got home, he sat down and put his leg up. He'd need to be well-rested for tomorrow.

WHY IN the heck he was so excited to be spending a day painting the walls of a bookshop, he had no idea. But Les hadn't slept well. Granted, that could have been because he couldn't get comfortable. When he did get to sleep, he kept waking up to check the clock. Finally he managed a few uninterrupted hours and didn't wake up until the alarm went off a little after eight.

His foot wasn't bothering him—a very good thing, considering he'd been on it a lot yesterday—so he went to the bathroom to clean up. He'd just finished brushing his teeth when his phone rang.

"Hey, Tyler," Les answered without looking. No one else called him at this time of day. Tyler, a good friend with a huge heart, worked at a clinic on the north side of Carlisle that provided free medical testing for various illnesses, many of a sexually transmitted nature. But if you called it an STD clinic, Tyler would flash a stare cold enough to freeze water at the equator.

"You're up." He was always too bright and cheerful for words. "Anthony and I are cooking out tonight, and we I thought you might want to join us. I didn't wake you up, did I?" He always asked that, but continued on before Les could answer. "It's just the two of us, and we haven't seen you since you crawled into your cocoon when you were injured and that bastard Chad left."

Les bristled at the mention of his ex. They'd been together two years, and Les had thought things were getting serious. Fat chance there. It turned out that while Les was giving away his heart and planning a future, Chad had been using his all over town, with any guy he could find. Les had had no idea that while he'd been putting in long hours so they'd have the resources to build a real life together, Chad had been using that time to go out and create a separate life of his own. He had taken advantage of the fact that Les was in a hospital bed and unable to walk to convey the news that he was leaving and following some guy to New York. Losing both his career and the man he had loved on the same day had nearly killed Les. But he'd survived. Maybe it was time he tried moving forward. "That would be nice. I'm helping a friend today with some painting and stuff. What time do you want me there?"

"A friend? What kind of friend? Is he the 'horizontal hula, get the hell out' kind of friend, or the 'kiss and make eyes at' kind of friend…? Or is he a friend-friend, like me? Though there's no one else like me in the whole world. Anthony likes to say that I'm one of a kind." Tyler paused for a split second. "Do you think he means that as a compliment or something else? I'm going to take it as a compliment because he loves me."

The planet was not ready for two people like Tyler. Les had met Tyler when he'd first joined the force. He'd been answering a possible assault call and arrived on the scene to find a guy on the sidewalk with Tyler sitting on top of him, glaring at the bigger man. At first Les had thought that Tyler was the suspect, but nope, Anthony had called the police because the man on the ground had tried to rob Tyler, who'd promptly laid him out with a kick to the nuts and a knee to the belly. All Tyler said when he got off the guy was that he needed to send a thank-you card to his self-defense coach.

"Can I talk now?" Les asked.

Tyler snickered. "You're so funny. Of course you can. Though most of the time, you're really quiet."

"Maybe that's because he can't get a word in edgewise," Les heard Anthony call out from somewhere behind Tyler. "Let the poor man talk. It's only eight thirty in the morning, and poor Les probably hasn't had his coffee yet. Besides, he doesn't need to tell you all about his friends and what he's doing."

"Of course he does. I'm his friend, and if this guy is the 'horizontal hula' kind of friend, then I have to make sure Les is being safe." He returned to the phone. "Stop in at the clinic today and pick up some condoms, just in case."

Les wasn't sure if he should laugh. "Tyler, he's a friend. I only met him the other day. His mom owned a bookstore downtown, but she just passed away. I'm going to help him repaint the inside so he can reopen."

"Sarah's place?" Tyler asked. "She's gone?" He was quiet for a few seconds, and Les wondered if Tyler had been close to her. In the years he'd known him, Tyler was never, ever quiet. "That's too bad. My nanna used to take me there to buy me books. I still have some of them in a box somewhere...." There was a pause, and Les thought he'd heard him swallow. But seconds later, Tyler was back. "Still, you should get some condoms, just in case."

"I don't think that's going to be necessary. Dex is super hot. He's been making movies in Hollywood." Les was a small-town guy. He knew who he was, but he also knew that guys like Dex didn't usually go for men like him.

"Why not? Because of your foot?" He made a pffft sound. "Please. You're really smoking. If I didn't have Anthony, and if he wasn't the hunk of hunks who gets my motor running without even trying, I'd definitely be interested in you." He plowed on. "I mean it, you're a catch. You'll figure out what you want to do and you'll be great at it. I just know you will. Sometimes I have a feeling about that sort of thing, and I'm getting one right now."

"Tyler, you need to get to work. You were asking poor Les about dinner. Remember?" Les heard Anthony's voice in the background. Sometimes Les thought Tyler's partner was a saint, putting up with Tyler's frenetic energy and propensity for putting his foot in his mouth. Still, Tyler was genuine and caring—a true friend. "Oh, yeah. Will you come to dinner? Bring your friend too. I think that would be great. Then I can ask him what his intentions are."

The phone shuffled. "Please bring your friend if you want, and I promise that Tyler will behave himself." Anthony was a sweet man who adored Tyler to death. Where Tyler was over the top, Anthony was sedate. Together they were perfect for one another.

"I'll ask him if he wants to come," Les agreed.

"Good. Now go ahead and start your day. Tyler needs to get his tight little butt to work, and I have to go into my office so I can actually get something done today." As well as working at the clinic, Tyler was also a counselor at Dickinson College. Anthony, on the other hand, had a column with several sports magazines, so he spent a lot of time in front of the television. Les would never have guessed that the two of them would be so perfect for each other. But they loved each other deeply and seemed to be exactly what the other needed. "Come to dinner, and I'll try to keep Tyler's grilling to a minimum. And bring your friend if he wants to come… and if you think Tyler won't be able to scare him away."

"Hey… I'm nice." Tyler must have snatched the phone back.

"And scary as all hell. But I'll see if he wants to come." Les hung up, then finished getting ready before driving over to the store and parking behind it. He wanted to save his energy—and his foot— for helping Dex, and he figured they would be coming and going by the back door.

Les knocked on the back door and waited for Dex. When he didn't hear any movement inside, he knocked again. Just as Les was about to go around to the front, Dex opened the door. "Hey. Come on in." Les went inside, and Dex closed and locked the door behind him. "I got the paint this morning." He led the way into the front, where the shelves had been pulled out for access. Fortunately the wild colors didn't extend all the way down the walls.

"You got a lot done already," Les said as he checked out a gallon of paint. "Light butter yellow."

"Yeah. I liked your suggestion. It will keep the store bright, and it's not as hard on the eyes as some of the colors in here. I also got a colored primer that we can put on first to keep the old paint from bleeding through." He pulled out a roll of plastic, and the two of them got busy covering everything. "You know you don't have to do this."

Les shrugged, trying to decide what he wanted to say. "I have a lot of time on my hands. I've been really active my whole life, but once I got injured, I ended up spending a lot of time at home in front of the TV. I used to run half-marathons on the weekends. Now I'm on disability for the foreseeable future. I could sit at a desk and do paperwork, but then one of the other guys would have to give up his spot. So instead, I spend a lot of time sitting at home."

"I appreciate the help," Dex said with a huge smile that left Les with a dry throat. Something about Dex made his heart skip a beat. Again, he really hoped that there was nothing going on with the store. Yeah, he'd had his suspicions about what Sarah might have been doing to keep things running, but the more time he spent with Dex, the more he wanted his suspicions to be wrong. "There will be some ladder work, but I can do that. I figured I'd cut in and you could roll the paint. I picked up an extendable pole, so you can stay on the floor and still reach the whole way."

"Sounds good," Les said, swallowing hard to try to moisten his mouth.

"There's a cooler on the counter over there. Just help yourself. And the bag has some sandwiches and things that Jane made."

"How is she doing?" Les opened the can of primer, stirred it a little, and poured the paint into the roller pan, then tipped some into a red handheld cup for Dex, who climbed the ladder and started edging at the ceiling.

"Pretty well. I think she's a little lost, but what else could I expect? Mom was healthy up until she had the stroke, so all of this is really sudden for both of us. At least all the arrangements had been made, so Jane didn't have to make a ton of decisions."

"How long had they been together?" Les got his roller ready and followed behind Dex, covering the old color as best he could. The primer spread well, but the scent grew overpowering as they finished the first wall and started on the next.

"About ten years. My father died a year or so before they met. It was a tough time for her, and she had to come to terms with loss as well as falling in love with another woman. But Mom did it in her usual fashion, especially once she realized how she felt about Jane." Dex climbed the ladder again, and Les couldn't help admiring how well his old jeans framed his butt. Dex had an incredible physique: wide shoulders, narrow hips, and a tight butt that Les would love to grab hold of and not let go. He shook his head, trying to drive away those thoughts.

Les knew he was nice-looking, and he'd never had any trouble attracting guys, but that had all changed with the accident. Now he needed help to get around most of the time, so dancing all night was out of the question. He could go without the cane, but using it took just enough weight off his foot that he could be a little more active.

Les was getting so tired of sitting at home all the time. He wasn't going to be able to run again or spend hours hiking in the woods anymore. He could walk over level terrain, but that was about it. And even then, after about a half an hour, his foot started to ache. The doctors had told him that this was likely the way his life was going to be from now on. They had done what they could to save his foot, but the damage the bullet had done would be with him for the rest of his life.

"Was it hard for you to get used to your mom being with Jane?" Les asked, shifting his weight to his good foot while he methodically rolled on the primer. Every now and then, he glanced over at Dex, unable to stop watching him.

"At first. I knew I was gay, but I didn't understand how my mom could go from my dad to Jane. I think I was pretty nasty at first. I regret that now, because I know it really hurt Mom. Jane was stubborn and refused to allow my bad behavior to affect anything. She remained the way she is—kind and loving—and without me really thinking about it, she won me over." He finished the ceiling edge on that wall and stepped off the ladder to fill in the corner. "I'm ashamed that I acted that way now. Jane was so good for my mom, and they were good to one another. Mom was happy, and that was what should have mattered."

"I can understand you resenting her, though. You were barely an adult yourself and still hurting because you'd just lost your dad."

"Yeah, but Mom was hurting too. I should have looked at things from her perspective." He finished edging the wall. "Now Jane is family, just like Mom was, and I don't think I could imagine not knowing her. Mom was funny and could be quirky." He motioned around the store. "Jane is levelheaded and steady. Together, they were amazing." He turned away, and Les saw him wipe his eyes.

"If you want a laugh and some insight into my mom's sense of humor, go take a peek in the bathroom."

Les finished the wall and went back. He stepped inside and laughed. "The Alice going down the hole is priceless. You must have had an amazing childhood." He returned and started on the next wall. Les was about half done with the first coat, but his foot was already aching.

He and Dex talked until the first coat was done, and then Les pulled over a chair, sat down, and elevated his foot. He gave a sigh of relief. Dex brought him a bottle of water and set the cooler between them.

"I'm going to prop open the back door before we end up high as kites." He left, and Les looked around.

If he was going to do some snooping, where would he start? It was unlikely that anything illegal would have been going on out here. He'd have to take a look in the back room somewhere. Not that Les had a clue where to start. And he didn't want to upset Dex. What if he found something? Did it really matter now? Dex's mother was dead, and whatever she might have been doing, it'd have passed on with her. It wasn't like Dex was responsible for what his mother had done to keep the business running. It was probably best if he simply just let his suspicions go.

A breeze wafted past him, and Les breathed in the fresh air. "That feels good."

"There's a nice wind outside," Dex reported as he sat on the chair next to his, popping open the cooler again. Les closed his eyes and let the fresh air drift over him. "The primer is already half dry. It isn't going to take long before we can put on the paint." He smiled. "I think it's going to look nice."

"So, you've pretty much decided to stay and run the store? Or are you doing this in the hope that you'll be able to find a buyer?" Les asked as he glanced around the relatively small space.

Dex paused. "I don't know. There's nothing for me back in LA, and this just sort of fell in my lap. On one hand, I couldn't wait to get away from this town when I graduated from college, and the first thing I did was run away to Hollywood. I was going to make it big in the movies if it killed me. And that could still happen. I love acting, and I used to dream of being in the movies, but acting is harder work than most people realize, and just being able to get the roles I might actually want is mostly luck and who you know." He shrugged and put his feet up, taking a swig of water. While he drank, Les watched his throat work and wondered what those full lips tasted like, figuring a little fantasy wasn't going to hurt anyone. Hell, Les figured that fantasies were all he was going to have. So what the hell—he might as well have good ones.

Chapter 4

DEX LOWERED his empty water bottle and turned to Les. For a second he wondered if the guy was staring at him. Not that Dex minded. Les was a good-looking man, if a little ragged around the edges. Maybe that wasn't the best description. Les was definitely nice-looking. But he carried himself in a way that made him seem a little out of it. "Where was I?" Les fanned his face as Dex tossed the bottle toward the wastebasket. It sailed in, and he grinned.

"Keeping the store…," Les prompted.

"Right. Mom left me the whole building, not just the store. And right now, there's one vacant apartment I can move into while collecting rent from the other units. So the building can basically pay for itself. As for the store, I'm just not sure. Mom has had it as long as I can remember and always seemed to manage."

Les leaned a little closer. "You're thinking of staying, then. At least to see if you can make the business work?" He seemed to like that idea.

"I think so. I don't really have a reason to run back to California at the moment. There's no furniture in my apartment out there I'd want to keep, and I have a friend who will arrange to have the rest of my stuff shipped out here… just to stop me, permanently, from bugging him to find me work. He's also my agent, you see. My guess is that he'll do a dance of joy to get me off his books." Dex sighed because, sadly, that was true. The chances of him ever making it in Hollywood grew less likely each year. Maybe it had been a pipe dream all along. Here, with the store, he could make a living and build a future, if he threw himself into it. "Sometimes change is good." He pulled a bowl of fruit out of the cooler and offered some to Les. "What did you do… before you hurt your foot?"

Les hesitated. "I was in law enforcement. It was what I'd always wanted to do. I went to the academy and spent a few years on the force, though in the beginning, it was mostly traffic duty and things like that." Dex got the feeling that Les didn't mention what happened very often.

"You don't have to talk about it if you don't want to." Dex didn't want Les to feel pressured.

"It's okay. The therapist I worked with for a while told me I needed to open up." He shrugged. "Maybe she'd understand better if she'd been the one who had been shot and had his foot and career shattered by punks robbing a gas station out by the freeway for drug money. Those kids were so stupid…. Anyway, I just wasn't fast enough." He groaned. "I should have seen it coming and prevented the entire thing."

Dex could see the guilt written all over Les's face. But as far as he could see, it had been an accident. Shit happened. Lord, he should have that written on every single shirt he owned, in every color of the damned rainbow. "So you're clairvoyant? What about your partner?"

"Huh?" Les asked. "No, of course not. My partner took them into custody." He hesitated. "We hadn't been partners for very long, and I'd been doing most of the legwork." He sighed. "Let's just say he wasn't the best partner in the world. At least that was the way I remember it. The truth is, the details are still a little fuzzy. I keep going over what I know about what had happened after I had been shot, trying to make sense of everything."

"Then how could you possibly see it coming?" Dex asked simply. "I know." He got up and rummaged behind the desk until he found what he was looking for. Then he dropped the deck of Tarot cards into Les's lap. "Maybe you should use these. Mom swore by them and spent years learning to read the cards. This was her personal deck. She got them at an auction some years ago."

Les took the out of the package. "They're so thick." He gently rifled through the cards. "Why are some of them different?"

"She said that there were fifteen cards missing when she bought the deck, so she reproduced them herself, using the same back and drawing the faces of the cards herself to complete the deck. Mom said they were really special and old. She was tickled something fierce when she brought them home. Apparently she was the only one at the auction to know what they were." Dex had no clue what his mother had seen in them. All he knew was that they were among his mother's most prized possessions and that she used them in the store sometimes when customers requested a reading. "Mom kept them close to her, in a locked box behind the counter."

Les looked over the cards carefully. "Are they Italian?" Dex nodded as Les handed them back. "They're beautiful. You should display them somewhere. Maybe under glass on the counter where you can see them too. It'll be another way of keeping your mom close to you."

Dex put them back into the box with tissue and set them behind the counter once more.

"So what you're trying to tell me is that no one can see the future, right?"

"Ding, ding, ding. You get the prize. A piece of pineapple." Dex was trying to lighten the mood, and Les smiled. "If you want the grand prize, let me ask you this. At that crime scene, did you follow procedures?"

"Yes. I did what I was supposed to. There was an investigation, and I was completely cleared. But I still can't help feeling that I could have done more."

Dex smiled at him. "I bet you were—are—one hell of a cop." He patted Les's leg and then got to his feet. "I'm going to get the edging started on the next wall. You sit here for a while and let me get ahead of you." He got the paint ready and went to work.

"Do you know how long it's been since someone touched me?"

Dex stopped midstroke, his brush an inch from the wall.

"There's been no one since the accident."

Dex turned to where Les still sat, looking toward him, but Dex was pretty sure Les wasn't seeing him at all. "I had been seeing a guy for a few years—Chad. He was great—I thought—and things seemed serious between us."

"And when he heard you'd been hurt, he vanished?" Dex supplied.

"Kind of like that, yeah." Les slowly stood up. "I'm a cop, and I should be better at reading people… but I'm obviously not. And yeah, he disappeared like a fart in the wind. Didn't even come to see me in the hospital. Instead he just left me a voicemail that things weren't working out and that it was for the best. Blah, blah, blah."

"Did you know where he lived?" Dex turned back to the wall. "You know, you could... I don't know, run his plates and put out an AAB."

"That's APB, and why?"

Dex continued painting. "No, an AAB. All Asshole Bulletin. You could put one out to the entire human race so that everyone would know to avoid this guy. Where did you meet him?"

"At a club in Harrisburg. We danced and had a good time. Nothing too fast. I think that was why I liked him. We talked and had fun. We didn't even kiss until we went out on an actual date. I thought that I might have gotten lucky."

Dex nodded. "I get it. He was an asshole in disguise. Those are the worst."

Les laughed until he started coughing. "You have to be kidding."

"Nope. See, there are three kinds of assholes. The ones that are front and center are easy to spot. You know, the kind of guy who will steal your parking spot at the grocery store. They troll the clubs, but get nowhere because everyone knows they're an asshole. The only way they can get lucky is to hang around at closing time to pick up the drunks whose judgment is impaired."

When Les laughed, Dex continued. "Then there are the guys who only show their assholeness once you get them home, where they turn selfish and have an alarm clock on their dick. As soon as it goes off, they're out of there." Dex paused to let Les catch his breath. "The third and worst kind is the asshole in disguise. They lure you in and pretend to be nice and patient. Then as soon as something happens, they're out the door, gone, bye—and all you see is an ass in a pair of tight jeans turning the nearest corner."

"Oh God," Les gasped. "I've met all those guys more than once."

"We all have, honey. We all have. I've been to clubs on Melrose in LA, and as you sit at the table, it's all about trying to figure out which kind of asshole just walked by, because there, the assholes seem to breed like rabbits." He shrugged and wondered for the first time why he'd been holding on to his life out there so tightly. "It's a huge city, so everyone seems to move at an almost frantic pace." Dex finished edging the first wall, and Les got up to start rolling the paint.

"I like this color. It's bright, but soothing too," Les commented. "It's a real bookstore kind of color."

Dex stepped back and was pleased with what he'd chosen, though part of him felt as though he was covering up a part of his mother. But it was too late to stop. Besides, Dex had no intention of changing the one room that showcased his mother's personality best—the Alice in Wonderland bathroom. That was far too clever to touch. "It is." He climbed up the ladder to edge at the ceiling and around some of the irregularities of the building.

"Sorry. You were talking about the city," Les prompted.

"Yeah. I found it hard to meet people. I'd go to clubs, but it was hard to start a conversation with someone unless it revolved around sex and where to go… stuff like that. I like to dance, so I did a lot of that and got some attention." He climbed down and moved the ladder before going back to his edging. "But it became pretty apparent that if I wanted more, I would have to try to find it somewhere else. And I had no idea where to look."

"But did you like it?" Les asked.

"California has been my home for a while, and I had a few boyfriends, but nothing that lasted. I have an agent, but it didn't do much good. I don't seem to have whatever the casting agents are looking for. Maybe I never did. There's so much luck involved in breaking into the business. It's all about who you know or can get access to. Sure, some people are lucky and make it big. I'm just not sure I'm meant to be one of them." He climbed down and moved the ladder yet again. "I think maybe it's time I stop whining about what didn't happen out there and figure out a way to make things happen here." He had the chance to build something. His mother had seen to that, and Dex felt like he owed it to her to try. "So I think it's time for me to move on. I'm still young, and it isn't too late for me to find a new dream." After all, it certainly didn't look like the old one was going to materialize.

Dex finished the last of the high work on that wall and moved the ladder out of the way to do the rest.

"That's good," Les said rather flatly.

"Did I say something wrong?" Dex asked.

Les put the roller in the pan and left it there. "How can you give up on your dream so easily? I mean, it's nice that you want to stay here and keep what your mom started going. I guess I just don't understand." He picked up the roller again and started putting paint on the wall with more vigor than he had been using. "I still want to be a cop again. I'd give almost anything to make that happen. If you want to be in the movies...."

"I've tried for years. But it's not as if I'm giving up on my dream—I think it gave up on me. I went to more auditions than you can possibly imagine and received so much feedback, it's hard to keep it all straight. You're too young, you're too old, too tall... too short... too fair... too dark. You don't have the look. Your legs are too short. Your voice isn't deep enough. It's too deep. You name it, I've heard it." Dex put down his brush and perched on one of the ladder rungs. "I think there's only so much rejection a guy can take—especially for things that are out of his control. But even if I move here, I don't intend to give up acting. I'll still act, and maybe I'll be able to find some joy in it again." Dex had done a lot of thinking over the past few days and had come to the conclusion that maybe this was the best thing. "Mom gave me a chance at having something different."

"I just hate to see anyone give up on their dreams," Les said softly. "Or maybe it's that I don't want to give up on mine." He stood straighter and continued working. "I'd wanted to be a cop for as long as I could remember... and I had it, only to get it ripped away."

"Maybe that's the difference. I thought I had it so many times, but then it ended up as 'No, you're too....' Fill in the blank with whatever you want. Oh, I've been in movies and played victims and helped fill crowd scenes, stuff like that. I've seen plenty of stars. I wanted so badly to be one of those guys." The more Dex thought about it, the more his dream seemed selfish. "I wanted to be famous and make my mom proud of me." He held his head in his hands. "What I never stopped to think about was that my mom was always proud of me." A wave of grief washed over him, and Dex was suddenly tempted to push the ladder over and throw the paint against the damned wall. How could he not have seen that all these years? No matter how bad things were or what he did, his mom had been his cheerleader. Now she was gone, and Dex felt like he had wasted all that time—time he could have spent with her. "What do I do now?" It seemed like he was on this weird emotional hamster wheel that was completely out of control.

"I'm afraid I don't have any answers. There's nothing profound that someone can say to replace the kind of loss you've had."

"There has to be something," Dex said. "Some way to make me feel better."

Les continued rolling the paint. "All you can do is try to keep busy. When I got out of the hospital, I spent days wallowing in my own self-pity… okay, weeks. I knew the daytime television schedule better than the guide on the television. If it's Monday, it must be Hogan's Heroes, if it's Thursday, then it was The Nanny marathon. I did nothing, and the way I spent my days did nothing for me."

"Hogan's Heroes?" Dex felt himself smiling. "I haven't watched that in years."

"Well, I did, as well as a bunch of other mind-numbing TV shows, just to pass the time. Then I started going out. Most of the time it was just a walk to the corner and back because that was as far as I could go. I'd have lunch downtown and then go home. I sat alone, but there were people around me. Now and then I'd meet some of the guys for lunch. That was nice. But I did stuff, and now I do more." He continued rolling the paint slowly over the wall. "All I'm saying is that it gets better. I know it sounds cliché, but it's true. The loss becomes less acute and you learn to live without…."

"But in your case, nobody died," Dex said.

"My career did, just like that. I still get paid because the accident happened on the job, but that doesn't help me much. I still have trouble walking a block." He paused, and Dex got the feeling there was more to the story than Les was saying.

"When I was in the hospital, I got an infection that weakened my lungs too. When I get home this afternoon, I'll need to lie down because I'll have exhausted myself." He finished the one wall and started on the next. Dex got up and returned to his edging. "So yeah, no one died, but the process and the grief are the same. I lost something that was very important to me, part of the way I identified myself. So yeah, I grieved, and I know what you're going through."

"But…."

Les stopped, then turn to him, his gaze hard. "There are no buts. Your grief isn't superior to mine just because someone died. It's all how you feel about it. You had your mom for almost thirty years, I'm guessing. She supported you and she even provided you with a potential future. So grieve for her, by all means. But your mom is still here. We're painting over her awful taste in wall colors, but this store will always have some part of her in it." Les smiled. "That is, as long as you keep that bathroom."

Some of the darkness that seemed to have descended over him lifted a little. "I know you're right. But it's so hard...."

Les set down the roller and slowly came over. His foot must have been hurting, judging by his halting steps. "Maybe you need to give yourself a little time. You just had your mom's funeral yesterday. No one bounces back quickly from that. It took me weeks to figure out a way ahead. You don't have to do everything in fast-forward."

Before Dex realized it, Les had him in a tight embrace. It felt so good to be held. Forgetting about the brush in his hand, he barely avoided getting a gob of paint on Les's back. Fortunately for his shirt, he pulled it away just in time. Dex held his breath for a few seconds and then released it, relaxing into the embrace.

"It's okay to take things one step at a time and grieve for her. There isn't a time limit."

"I guess."

"And you know that it's okay to be sad sometimes. This isn't an easy road, and the grief will hit you when you least expect it. But things will get better and you'll figure out how to go on with your life." He released him.

Dex nodded, wiping his eyes and feeling a little like a dork. He turned back to the wall. "Do you need to sit and rest your foot?"

"I'll be okay. We're getting close to being done. Let's just finish." Les returned to painting, and Dex finished up the last of the cutting in, with Les right behind him completing the rolling.

Once they were done, they stepped back. The walls were bright and cheerful, the light through the front windows bouncing off the walls. The green carpet didn't seem quite as garish now. Dex had thought of trying to replace it, but maybe he could bring in some rugs to cover it up and to help delineate the spaces. "I like it. Sorry, Mom."

"Do you really think she'd be upset?" Les asked.

Dex shook his head. "I think she'd say she liked the color, but it was a little sedate and that it needed some companions. Or maybe some chickens or foxes." He explained about the kitchen wallpaper, and Les howled with laughter. "Mom had her own taste, and it made her unique." Dex checked his watch. "Come on. This needs to dry, so we might as well clean everything up. It's a little after one. I'd say the least I can do is buy you lunch."

"That would be nice." Les sat down with a sigh.

"Did you stand too much?" Dex asked.

"I just need to get off it for a little while." He propped his foot up on one of the boxes and leaned back. "It's the thing I hate the most. I can walk okay and stand, but if I'm upright for too long, the blood seems to settle there. To ease the pressure, I have to sit and elevate it."

"Then stay there, and I'll wash everything out and we can go." Dex gathered the supplies and headed for the back room. Off near the bathroom was an old wash sink he could use to clean the supplies. He kicked a box out of the way, dropped everything in the sink to soak, and flapped his hands to shake off the water before opening the heavy box.

"What the heck?" He squinted at the contents, wondering if he was seeing right.

The box contained a bunch of miscellaneous paperbacks. He pulled one out and opened it. "Huh?" The inside of the book had been hollowed out. He picked up another one, and it was the same way. There were probably a dozen books in there, and each one had been ruined… or whatever this was. He put them back and set the box aside before finishing with the brushes and pans.

The roller he squeezed the paint out of, wrapped in plastic, and tossed away. The rest he cleaned and set to dry before placing the box near the back door. On his way out, he figured he'd take a paperback home to Jane to see if she knew anything about it. Why would his mother have modified a bunch of books so things could be hidden in them?

Shit, maybe there were other things scattered throughout the store. Should he take a closer look at the shelves? Dex wiped his hands, shaking his head. That was a stupid idea. He'd keep Les waiting. But maybe he should take a look at the books behind the counter.

"Do you need some help?" Les asked.

Dex closed up the box. "I'll be just a minute." He finished up and left a book on top of the box so he could grab it when he returned. Why he was so jumpy all of a sudden, Dex wasn't sure. Maybe it was the fact that Les had been a police officer, and something about this situation didn't feel right to him. Or smell right, for that matter. Dex sneezed twice and returned to where Les waited.

"Are you ready? I think I can leave everything as it is until tomorrow. The paint will be dry by then, and I can put the shelves back before going through everything to see what's here and how I can stage a grand reopening."

Les lowered his foot, and Dex grabbed the cooler and snack bag and guided Les outside. He picked up the hollowed-out book and placed it in the bag before locking the back door. "How about Café Belgie? They have a great lunch, and I think we've earned their frites. At least, I hope they're still as good."

"I love those," Les said with a groan.

Dex knew Les's foot had to be hurting. "My car is right over there." He pointed to his rental. He beeped open the door and put the things he was carrying into the trunk while Les got in. Then he climbed in as well and they were on their way. The restaurant was only a few blocks away. His karma must have been good, because he found a parking spot right in front.

"Hey, Les," the server said when they walked inside. He gave Les a quick hug. Then he turned to Dex. "I'm Billy. Welcome."

"Dex."

"Sarah's son," Les supplied.

Billy's expression saddened. "I'm sorry about your mom. She was a great lady. I always took our boys to her shop. We were just in there last week to look around. I always loved that place." He showed them to a table. "She was a fun lady and she always had time to chat. I swear she sold more books that way. I'd come in to look around and end up leaving with a few novels she'd recommended. We're going to miss her."

"Dex is going to reopen it," Les said as they sat down. "We were just doing some repainting."

"Not the bathroom?" Billy asked hurriedly. "That was one of Sarah's most amazing creations. She worked on that for a long time."

"No," Dex answered. "I'd hate myself if I ever hurt Alice and her friends. But the rest of the store needed some freshening up." It was funny how everyone in town seemed to know about the store bathroom. "I'm hoping to reopen this weekend. I'm not sure what sort of festivities I can put together, but I want to do something to remember Mom."

"Then we'll be there. She was quite a lady." Billy handed them menus before leaving the table. Dex and Les talked over what they wanted and placed their orders when Billy returned.

Dex watched Les, trying to think of something to say. But he was out of small-talk starters, and after working all morning, he was tired. "I'm sorry. My conversation skills seem to have flown the coop."

Les smiled. "It isn't necessary to fill every minute with talk. When I joined the force, Harry, my first mentor, had this thing where he hated silence. He used to talk about anything, even the trees as we passed them."

"The trees?" Dex asked.

"Yeah. He had this pet peeve. See, in town there's a shade tree commission, but they only regulate what homeowners can do with the street trees. As for the others… well, they hate to cut trees down, so we end up with some of the weirdest-shaped things you have ever seen. He called Carlisle the Borough of Frankentrees. So when we'd drive through town, if it was quiet, he'd point out all the weird ones. Like the maple on North that has been trimmed so many times by the power company that the canopy is actually bowl-shaped. In some places there's only half a tree, but because it's alive, the commission won't let them cut it down and replace it." Les grinned and groaned at the same time. "God…."

"You mean running on about the trees when your story was about how you sometimes like it quiet?" It was too much fun not to tease him a little.

"Okay. So I can run on about things just a little bit. I think I caught it from Harry. I sort of learned to talk so I could get a word in.

Otherwise I swear he would talk for eight hours straight." Les leaned over the table. "He would start a discussion on a topic, like, say, the danged trees, and then we'd get a call and he would be all business. But once the call was over, he'd pick up the tree thing without missing a beat." Les drank some of his water and set down the glass. He paused, and Dex wondered if it was his turn. "What?" Les asked. "I'm trying to be quiet and not prattle on."

"I like listening to you talk." Maybe that was it… or maybe Dex was just destined to have motormouths in his life. That wasn't such a bad thing, because there were times when he just wasn't up to speaking. "Your voice is really mellow and soothing. But I bet when you're in full-on cop mode…." Dex shivered and wondered where that had come from. He held Les's gaze, and neither of them spoke for a while. Then Dex leaned over the small table and, when Les didn't pull away, touched their lips together.

A soft gasp sounded from off to the side, and Dex drew back, thinking that they had offended someone with their PDA. Instead he saw Billy standing near the server station, smiling, his hands together. Then the man turned away and hurried toward the kitchen.

Les didn't sit back, and Dex had no intention of moving. He allowed his hand to slide along Les's.

Les nodded toward Billy. "He's been trying to get me to date for months, and I've resisted. So now I'm sure he's over the moon and is likely, at this very moment, telling his husband what he just saw. Don't be surprised if champagne and a three-piece band suddenly make an appearance." Les snorted.

Dex once again leaned across the table. It seemed he had the green light, and this time, instead of worrying so much about the kiss itself, he got to actually taste the slightly salty sweetness of Les's lips.

"You two," Billy said. "You look so—"

"If you say cute, you die." Les scowled at Billy, who rolled his eyes.

"I was gonna say hot. Really hot. But since you decided to be Mr. Snarky McMeanie, I guess I could leave your food at that table over there to get cold, if you want." When he turned away, Les groaned. That seemed to be Billy's cue to place the plates in front of them. "I'd never do that. Darryl would be upset. And when it comes to his food…." He fanned himself. "I just love me a hot chef." With that little announcement, Billy bounded away.

"Is he always like that?" Dex asked.

"God, no. Billy is the consummate professional most of the time. He manages the entire front of the restaurant, seating people and overseeing the waitstaff. And he keeps things at home with Darryl running smoothly. He's a happy man, and he wants the rest of the world to be as happy as he is. I suppose there's nothing wrong with that."

Dex grabbed a fry and popped it into his mouth. He loved frites, with their soft inside and crunch on the outside. "Then why do you look like someone kicked your puppy?"

Les sighed. "Look at me. I can't stand for more than a few hours without pain. Today was about the longest I've been on my feet in months, and I know I'm going to pay for it tonight." He nudged his pot of mussels away.

"Your foot isn't who you are," Dex said. He was trying to understand how Les felt and was honestly coming up empty. This was something he had little experience with.

"No. But it affects whoever I'm with." He scooped out a shell and ate the mussel from inside. "Okay, so let's say that I meet someone. He's about my age, healthy, and vibrant. What am I going to be except a millstone around his neck? I can't go hiking or even take a long walk."

"If someone cares about you, they're going to accept you for who you are." Dex realized how stupid he sounded as soon as the words crossed his lips.

"And what am I?" Les whispered. "I'm a broken former cop who can barely take care of himself. I spend most of my time sitting in a damned chair because I have to keep my foot up. The doctors say that it's unlikely that it will ever improve."

Dex was stunned into momentary silence. "Doctors don't know everything. And it's your foot—not your mind or your heart." He met Les's glare with one of his own. "I don't know how you feel, and I wish I could do something to help you." The thing was that he was out of his depth with this. Dex's instinct was to try to solve the problem, but this was out of his control. It was out of Les's too, and maybe that was the issue.

"Yeah. But let me ask you something. Why would a vital young guy want to date someone who can't even walk two blocks to a restaurant when he could have his pick of anyone who could run a marathon if they wanted?"

Dex cut into his steak. "I don't know." He leaned over the table. "Maybe some of us just know how we want to spend our time and who we want to spend it with. Maybe this half-marathon guy is pretty cool, but so is the guy who offered to help someone he'd only met a couple of times paint the inside of their bookstore."

"But I want more…."

Dex sighed. "Hey, I'm the king of wanting more. I moved out to Hollywood and lived in a postage-stamp-sized apartment I could barely afford in order to chase a dream with a minuscule chance of success. I waited tables and did small theater in the hopes I'd be discovered. I took jobs in clubs and places where I might be seen, and all I got were tire marks on my back and ass and flat feet from pounding the pavement all the time. So I know about wanting more. God, I know it so damned well." The years of frustration and the grief of the last few days took over, and all Dex saw was black. It was almost as if the sun had disappeared behind a cloud. "But I can't have it. At least, I can't have any of that, no matter how hard I might try." He took a deep breath and tried to will the darkness away. "I'm sorry." He pushed away his plate of steak. "This doesn't have anything to do with you."

"Maybe it has something to do with both of us. Maybe we're both just in a shit place right now." Les returned to his lunch, eating slowly. This time the silence was heavy and lingered forever.

Finally Dex had to say something. "Or maybe we both have some baggage we need to deal with."

Les snorted. "You can say that again."

"But everyone has baggage."

"Unfortunately, mine is the size of a Louis Vuitton trunk, packed with useless crap and weighed down with concrete guilt," Les quipped.

"If that's the case, then mine is the transatlantic baggage of a fifties debutante planning her coming out before the queen," Dex countered.

"Debra Messing with all that light blue luggage stacked on the airport cart in The Wedding Date," Les added, upping the ante.

"Is that so? How about Scarlett O'Hara with Rhett Butler when they have to have a separate cabin for everything on their way to New Orleans?" He cocked his eyebrow, and Les's mouth hung open.

"Damn, you win. You have more than I do." Les bowed slightly and waved his hand.

"Damned straight. I've spent years building up all that weight. Maybe I should be on Hoarders, the emotional baggage episode."

"Either that or you could do an exposé—My Life as a Wannabe Porn Star," Les added with a grin, and Dex followed, pulling back his lunch and letting most of the darkness go. It still seemed to hang around the edges of the afternoon, but Les's smile and his laughter made things better.

They finished their lunches, and Dex sat back in the chair. He was full and declined Billy's offer of dessert. "What do you have for the rest of the day?"

"I'm going to go put my foot up for a while, and later tonight I'm going to dinner with some friends." He took a deep breath. "I told them I was spending the day with you and… well… they told me to ask if you wanted to come. You don't have to if you don't want to. But when I told Tyler I was meeting a friend, his curiosity went into overdrive. He and his partner, Anthony, are really great guys, and they've been there for me since the accident. A lot of my other friends simply faded into the background because my life changed so damned much. But Tyler and Anthony understood and stuck by me. I met them soon after I moved here for work, and we've been solid ever since."

Dex thought about his empty dance card.

"It's up to you. You don't have to come," Les said quickly. "I mean… it was probably a stupid idea."

Dex touched Les's hand, and it acted like an Off switch. He grew quiet and met Dex's gaze. Damn, he could get lost in those incredibly expressive and deep eyes. "I'd like to go. If you give me the address and tell me what time they want us there, I'll be happy to meet you and your friends for dinner. Jane is getting together with some of her friends tonight too. Apparently there's a group of them who have made it their business to keep her calendar filled for a while."

"Awesome." Les gave him the address. "They said to be there about six."

"That's south of town."

"Near the Walmart. It's the street that doesn't have a stoplight. At least that's how I remember it." The light danced in Les's eyes.

"Then I'll see you there."

DEX WASN'T sure how he should dress, so he went middle of the road, choosing a polo and khaki pants. Then he left the house and drove to the address he'd been given. It was a little after six when he walked up the manicured, flower-lined walk to the front door. Dex rang the bell, and a few seconds later the door opened.

"You must be Dex. I'm Tyler." A slim man a little over five feet tall looked him over from head to toe. "I'm glad you could come. Les was telling us all about you, and let me say that I approve." He stepped back as Les approached.

"Tyler, don't scare him off."

"Oh, please. This adorable-as-a-teddy-bear man here doesn't look like he'd be that easily driven off." Tyler grinned at Dex, who took his comment as a compliment. "Come on in. We're out back. Anthony is doing his manly duty at the grill, and I'm mixing some drinks. Les and I were about to have a cosmo, but you can have whatever you want."

Dex smiled. "A cosmo sounds great." Then he turned to Les and took his hand. "You look very nice," Dex whispered.

"So do you," Les said softly, a touch of heat in his eyes.

Tyler clapped his hands. "You two couldn't look cuter together if I had picked you out myself."

"Tyler," Les said gently. "Can you dial it down just a little?"

"No, he can't," a deeper voice said.

"Hello," Dex said, turning to greet the newcomer.

"I'm Anthony. It's best if you just let Tyler wind down some. He's been trying to fix Les up with someone for months." He extended his hand for Dex to shake and then slipped an arm around Tyler's waist. "You know, honey, it takes some people a few minutes to get used to being in your blinding light."

Tyler smiled and leaned back into Anthony's embrace. They were adorable. Then Tyler nodded. "Okay, let me finish making the drinks and I'll join you all on the patio."

Anthony gave Tyler a squeeze before letting him go, then led the way through the house.

Dex looked around, admiring the place. It was of the same era as his mother's, but this one had been painted and decorated in a very modern style that took its cues from the original architecture. It was really pleasant and looked comfortable.

The backyard was beautiful in its simplicity, with beds of bright flowers and a pergola-shaded flagstone patio. "Please have a seat. Tyler will be right out. Right now I need to check the grill."

"Can I help?" Dex asked.

"I have it, thanks." He hurried away, leaving Dex and Les alone.

Dex looked around, feeling a little out of place. These were Les's friends. Maybe he should have simply stayed home. "How long have you known Les and Anthony?"

"About four years, I guess. Dickinson College has quite a few programs, and most of them are open to the public. I met Tyler at one of the events there." He looked up as Tyler carried a tray of pink drinks and set it on the table before handing them out.

"He was so quiet, and you know I'm a huge motormouth. I walked up to him and asked him if he was having a good time," Tyler added.

"Then I had to step in to rescue him or else poor Les would have either run for the hills or arrested Tyler for disturbing the peace." Anthony cocked an eyebrow.

"I talk a lot. So what. You love me, and I have a lot to say." Tyler sat down. "I'm a counselor at the college. I help students who are having trouble adjusting to campus life." He sighed. "That's the easy part. I also work with students who are trying to overcome the trauma in their pasts. It can be heartbreaking…." Tyler sipped his drink and grew surprisingly quiet.

"Fifteen seconds," Les mouthed, and sure enough, the silent, sedate Tyler was gone almost as if someone had set a timer.

"We were having a party, and I invited Les, and we became friends after that." Tyler raised his glass and they clinked, with Anthony touching his beer bottle. Then he patted Tyler's shoulder and went to the grill.

He returned with a plate of shrimp on small skewers. "A few appies. We'll put the steaks on in a few minutes." Tyler passed out small plates, and Anthony sat down and joined them.

The food was great and the company lively. Dex felt himself relax as the conversation wore on. "Did you meet any big stars?" Tyler asked.

"A few. But I was usually in the background. They're busy and have jobs to do, so we're told not to disturb them. Besides, how much time do you get to talk when you're playing corpse number three? I got really good at lying still and appearing to not breathe." He shrugged.

"Les said that you're going to reopen the bookstore downtown," Tyler commented, his gaze darting to Les and then to Anthony. He might even have tensed. Dex wasn't sure.

"Yeah. Mom passed away and left it to me."

Anthony nodded. "We saw that, and we're really sorry. Your mom was someone special here in town. Both Tyler and I went to the store when we were kids."

"She used to read stories on Saturdays, and Mom would take me down and then she'd buy me a few books. I don't think I've been inside in a while, though," Tyler added a little guiltily.

"That's the problem. It's so easy to buy whatever you want from Amazon or Barnes and Noble that most people don't bother to visit a bookstore anymore. Brick-and-mortar stores can't compete when it comes to inventory. Right now I'm looking over the accounts and trying to work out ways to keep the store going. Mom was doing okay, it seems, but… well, we'll see once I can open again."

"Anthony and I will stop in," Tyler said.

"I'll be open this weekend. I have to do some cleaning and get everything back in place, but I should have things set up by then." He was determined to honor his mother's legacy. He just hoped he could keep it going.

"Awesome," Tyler said enthusiastically. "Les, do you think you could help me in the kitchen a minute?"

"Of course," Les agreed.

"Anthony, I'll have the steaks ready for you in a bit."

Tyler waited for Les. Dex got the idea that Tyler didn't need the help as much as wanted to talk. And by the way Tyler glanced at him, he knew he was the topic of conversation.

Chapter 5

TYLER GOT out the salad and set it on the counter. "You know, sometimes I wonder if I don't have fluff between my ears. Are you seeing Dex because he has the store now? I know you've been watching it. Are you using him as an in to find out what might have been going on in this Rear Window obsession of yours?" Tyler put his hands on his hips. "I hope not. I like him."

"So do I," Les countered, hating that Tyler was putting the picture together. After their phone call, he had thought that Tyler had forgotten what Les had shared with him months ago. "He's a good, caring person."

"But does he know that you suspected his mom of some kind of nefarious activity?" Tyler's accusatory tone set Les's back on edge. "Sarah was always so nice to everyone. I never understood the fixation that you had with the store." He stalked closer, which, given Tyler's stature, shouldn't have been threatening. But it was. He was usually so upbeat that when he scowled, it carried a great deal of weight. And when he crossed his arms over his chest, Les couldn't help taking a step back, cop or not.

"She had very few customers and still managed to keep that store in business. I watched it for a few days, and some people came and went, but they only bought a few books. How could that possibly have sustained the business, especially since most of the customers were little old ladies buying a paperback or two?" Les explained. "It seemed suspicious to me, and I'm a cop. I have to have answers when something doesn't smell right. And you know there was talk. The drug dealers we were chasing down when I got hurt.... I could never put my finger on it, but somehow what they were doing had something to do with the store. I just know it."

"So you got friendly with her son, even going so far as to help him paint the store, just so you could get inside and look around?" He huffed. "So what if Sarah had been doing something on the side to keep the store going? She was getting on in age. And you said yourself that the majority of her customers were older as well. What could she be doing? Smuggling Metamucil? Maybe she was pushing Viagra for their husbands?" Tyler rolled his eyes. "Do you think Dex knows anything about this?"

"Of course not," Les answered quickly.

"So you really like this guy?" Tyler asked, and Les nodded. "Then, in the words of the immortal RuPaul… don't fuck it up. Whatever was happening—if anything—died along with her."

"Dex is a nice guy, and I like him." He bit his lower lip.

"But let me guess, you can't let your suspicions go."

Les shrugged. "There's nothing I can do. I didn't see anything out of the ordinary when I was there. But that's not why I offered to help. I did that because Dex is nice and could be a good friend, and…."

"Yeah, yeah. Talk to the hand." Tyler made an exaggerated gesture. "I know you too well. But if you want my advice—though you probably won't take it—just let it go. Sarah is gone, and it's best to let her rest in peace." He smirked. "And in the meantime, you and her 'oh my God, he's gorgeous' son could rattle a few cages and treat each other to a few sleepless nights." Tyler fanned his face. "That guy is handsome as all hell, and he looks at you like you're someone special."

"He does?" Les asked.

Tyler stared at him as if he was stupid. "Duh. He has that soft, melty look in his eyes. I see it in Anthony all the time. He likes you." He wagged his finger. "So don't mess it up, or otherwise I'll start fixing you up with some of the guys I know from work. They're all counselors like me, but none of them have my sense of style or fabulousness." He sighed. "But they're nice, so they'll have to do."

Les put his hands in the air. "Fine. I'll stop being nosy as long as you agree not to try to fix me up with anyone. Now, what did you need me to bring back so we don't look like we were talking about Dex?"

"Can you carry this bowl with your cane?" Tyler handed him a dish, and Les half tucked it under his arm and made his way back toward the patio, with Tyler behind him holding a plate of steaks. He set the bowl on the table.

"Did you and Tyler have a good talk?" Dex asked, smiling. "I figured you needed a chance to catch up." He'd sat back in his chair, feet up on a stool with his drink in hand and looking every bit the movie star with nothing to do.

"We did. He needed a little help with one of the salads, but it's all set now."

"Once Anthony gets the steaks on, dinner will be about ten minutes." Tyler started to fuss with the table as he set everything out.

"He never sits still," Les told him. "Tyler is a lot of fun. He and I used to go dancing. Well, the three of us did. Anthony doesn't dance much, but Tyler and I used to heat up the dance floor. That was until…." Les hated that everything kept coming back to the accident. "I'm sorry."

"Hey," Dex said with a smile and drew him a little closer. "How about you stop worrying about what you can't do… at least for this evening." He snagged a kiss.

Tyler clanged the silverware, and when they turned, Les saw him do this little jig-type dance.

"What was that?" Anthony asked. "The meat is on and should be done in a few minutes."

"I'm happy. Look at them. They're so hot-cute," Tyler breathed.

"And you're acting like my busybody mother," Anthony growled.

Tyler shuddered and lightly smacked Anthony's shoulder. "You be nice. I am not at all like your mother, and don't you dare compare me to that horrid woman." He scowled.

"You don't get along with Darlene?" Les asked.

"The last time she was here, she referred to me as 'that fairy that Anthony is involved with' and then wondered when he was going to give me up for some big-bosomed girl she had picked out. I told her to get on her broom before someone dropped a house on her."

"You didn't," Dex asked with a smirk.

Anthony sighed. "He certainly did. My husband and my mother will never get along. And my mother can have an acid tongue. Tyler refuses to stand there and take it. Needless to say, my mother's visit lasted all of two minutes after that exchange."

"She deserved it," Tyler declared, his chin high. "One of my superpowers is to call a witch a witch, and that woman deserves a ride on a broom." He looked up from what he was doing. "Though she did… somehow… manage to raise Anthony right, so she can't be all bad. Just mostly."

"I better go check the meat," Anthony said as he hurried away.

"That woman is awful," Tyler said as soon as Anthony had gone. "She picks on him all the time, and he's way too nice to tell her where to get off. But I'm not going to take her kind of uppity crap. Whenever she says anything nasty to me, I just try to see what I can say to get her to leave as fast as possible. The witch line was a world record. She was gone in under two minutes." He seemed inordinately pleased with himself. "I better go see how long it'll be for the meat. I'll be right back."

"How much do you want to bet that the steaks will be overdone and Tyler will come back with dreamy expression on his face?" Dex asked.

Les snorted. "No bet. Those two will do just about anything to make each other happy. It's enough to make you believe in true love. Darlene Mason is notoriously controlling and is used to getting her own way. Her husband was mayor some years ago before he died of cancer."

"That must have been hard on Anthony, losing his father," Dex said.

"Anthony's father is still alive. It was his mother's second husband who died. Anthony's dad is a wonderful man, and Anthony is very close to him. They go fishing together and hunting in the fall. Sometimes they bring me some of the meat, and I cook it and have them—and Tyler, of course—over for dinner. Clyde is just lovely, and he's supportive and as open-minded as anyone could ask for. He visits regularly and is kind to everyone. Darlene, on the other hand, is a drive-by harpy." His expression hardened. "She only comes here when she wants something. Anthony's just too good a person to tell her to go away."

"I take it you've met her."

Les nodded. "She's like a hurricane, and I've been caught in her path a few times. Once I stopped her because she had run a red light. She thinks the rules don't apply to her." He leaned closer to Dex, drawn by his scent. "I gave her a ticket, mainly because of her attitude." Then Les kissed Dex, just because he could.

"The steaks are ready," Tyler called as he checked the table, his lips swollen. Les and Dex shared a glance and moved to the table for dinner.

THE MEAL was amazing—both Anthony and Tyler were great cooks. It was some of the best food Les had had in quite a while. "Thank you."

"Yes. Thank you for including me," Dex said as the last of the sun's rays slipped away. "I'm afraid I'm going to have to head out soon, though. I need to get to the store early in the morning. I still have to put everything back together and get cleaned up before the opening. I just wish I had something special that I could offer people when they stopped by. Or at least do something to make the place look different, more inviting."

"Change the windows," Tyler suggested. "You don't need to fill them with just books. There's that candy store down the way that always has amazing window displays. People stop to look and usually end up going inside."

"That's a good idea. Maybe I can find some things in the back. Mom never threw anything out, and there's an area above the book bins in the back that I haven't checked out yet. Maybe I'll find some interesting things there." The interest in Dex's eyes reflected the fire from the portable firepit that Anthony had brought over. "I think Mom used to have some stuffed toys around. She used them for story time. Who knows? They might still be there."

"I'd say to do one window for the kids, but if you have enough stuff for both of them… maybe you should do both, especially if you can make the adults sentimental," Tyler offered. "Sometimes that's all it takes for people to stop and come inside. Sarah was getting older, so she usually just put books in the windows. Maybe something new will help."

"I suppose," Dex said softly. "I keep wondering how Mom kept the place going all these years."

Les leaned closer. "I'm sure she had loyal customers." He knew that was true. He'd seen the same people coming in regularly from his front window. "What you need to do is find out what they want, make sure you have it, and then try things that could attract new customers. I think that starts with getting people in the door and then talking to them. They'll tell you what they want if you listen."

"That's really true," Anthony said as they all got up.

Les had been able to rest his foot on one of the footstools, and it felt pretty good. "I should head home and try to get some rest. I haven't been sleeping very well lately," he admitted. "But this has been the best day I've had in quite some time." He got to his feet and hugged Tyler and Anthony tightly.

Dex thanked them again, and they shared hugs as well before the two of them left the house and headed down the walk.

It was dark, and Les started slightly when Dex's hands slid over his cheeks. "I want to ask you to come home with me, but I think it's best if we wait." He kissed him, and Dex held Les tightly. "I've always been someone who goes after what he wants. But it's too soon for us." He ran his hands down Les's back, and Les groaned softly. It felt so good to be held, to be desired, and there was no doubt that Dex wanted him. He felt it easily, insistently.

"Dex... I...."

"My mother used to say that the best things in life are worth waiting for, and I think I can put you in that category." The roughness in Dex's voice created shivers that ran up his spine. "Friday I'm opening the store. I'm closing at eight. Would you like to go to dinner afterwards?"

Les nodded, his mouth dry as Dex's hot breath danced over his skin. "I think I'd really like that."

"Excellent. Do you want to meet at the store?" Dex pulled back a little, the warmth of his body slipping away. Les nodded again, his pulse racing. He wanted to hold Dex and just tell him that they could go to his place. But Les liked that Dex wanted to wait. It made things better. And the truth was, if he wanted something different from what he'd had in the past, he had to break those behavior patterns. He had never been good at waiting.

"I'll meet you on Friday," Les said.

"Then come on. I'll see you home."

They walked to the cars and got inside. The ride didn't take long, and once they were parked, they said good night. Dex got back into his car, and Les watched until he waved and turned the corner, then headed up to his apartment.

LES SPENT the next few days doing his best not to watch the bookshop across the street out his front windows. Whatever Dex was doing, he didn't need Les stalking him. Not that he could see much. Dex had put paper up in the windows to create some mystery, and Les was more than a little curious about what he had come up with.

"I see Dex took my advice," Tyler said Thursday night when he called. "I went by the store and the windows were covered." He chuckled. "I peeked through the cracks in the paper, but I couldn't see very much. He's been making changes, though. I guess I'm going to have to wait with bated breath, just like the rest of the town, to see what he's done."

"I know. I can see the store from my place, remember?"

"Did you see the story in the Sentinel? It was about Sarah and how Dex is keeping the store going to honor her memory. It was a nice piece. I hope it helps Dex's business. Or at least creates some interest. Anthony and I were going to drop by after work tomorrow to see the place. Are you going to come with us?"

"I'll head over closer to closing. Dex and I are going to dinner." Les hoped there would be reason to celebrate.

"I see," Tyler said, and Dex could almost see him grinning. "Does this mean that you're going to go from friends to boom-chicka-mow-mow friends?" He was having way too much fun with this.

"What are you, twelve?"

"It's just that it's been a long time," Tyler said.

Les groaned. "How do you know how long it's been since I was with someone?" he demanded, more harshly than he intended.

"That," Tyler returned reasonably. "There is no way that someone as grumpy as you get sometimes could be getting any on a regular basis." He actually laughed.

"Don't you have to go to work or something?" Anything. This wasn't a subject he intended to talk about. If things did get intimate between him and Dex, then that would be between them. His personal life was not for public consumption. Tyler was many things, but beyond his professional bubble, the man was anything but circumspect. Les assumed that at work he understood discretion and what was private, but outside of that, everything seemed to be fair game. Honestly, if he wanted to discuss his sex life, he was more likely to talk to Anthony. Though the idea of talking about it at all was enough to make his arms itch. "Just let things be, please. I don't know what's going to happen." Dex's words on the sidewalk had rolled through his mind for much of the night, and he still had this excited energy running through him.

"Okay. I'll be good for now. But you know I'm going to want details," Tyler said. "And I can't wait to see what you look like once you've been sexed up." The man had no shame at all. "I bet you're as cute as a little bunny."

Les mock-growled.

"Oh… a teddy bear. Okay. I can work with that. And I bet Dex can too."

He rolled his eyes and groaned. "God, please just let it go."

"I would, but I can tell you're trying to stop yourself from laughing. You know it's okay to be happy. No one is going to pull the rug out from under you just because there's a little pleasure or happiness in your life." Sometimes, when Tyler's counseling background came through, he was way too insightful. "I know it's been hard for you." He suddenly seemed serious. "But bad things are not going to happen if you let yourself be happy."

"How do you know that?" Les asked.

"Okay, maybe I don't. But the world doesn't work that way. You don't have to pay for being happy with really bad stuff. I know you had the job you'd always wanted and then it got taken away. Shit happens. I wish it didn't. But that doesn't mean you stop living, loving, or letting people into your life."

"I'm doing my best."

"Good. Anthony and I are going to visit the store at six. We'll stop by and pick you up on our way. I read in the paper that there would be refreshments and some special activities for children and adults."

Les knew he'd only invite more trouble if he argued.

"Please."

Holy crap. Tyler did a lot of things, but saying please wasn't one of them. He usually got his own way simply by wearing whoever he was talking to down. "Okay. I'll meet you out front at six and we'll walk over together. But I don't want to be in the way. Promise me that if the place is packed, we'll leave and return closer to closing. We can have drinks here or something." If the store was empty, then they could stay and make it seem fuller. "I want this to be a success for him."

"I've told everyone at the college that with the store reopening, we should be supporting it instead of the large chains or else it isn't going to be around for long." Les could almost see Tyler's smug smile.

"I bet you did."

"Of course. Dex is a friend now, and we support our friends. Brick-and-mortar stores are a dying breed, so unless we want a town with nothing but online shopping for our books, we need to support them."

"Yes, we do. I'll see you then."

Les sat down on his chair. He could already tell that the day was going to be warm, and he wished he had an air conditioner in this room. He kept one in the bedroom, but it wasn't big enough to cool the entire apartment. He'd thought of getting another one, but the only window he could place it in was the front one, and he didn't want to lose the light... or the view. In the end, he closed the door to the kitchen and dining area before opening the bedroom door. Since the rooms were small, he could cool this space, and that would have to do for his day inside.

THE SUN was still bright and the temperature was near ninety degrees outside. Fortunately he had been able to spend the day in cool air. Les dressed in light clothes, watching for Anthony's car. When he saw it, he grabbed his cane and slowly descended the stairs to street level. That was one of the hardest things he did all day. Les was determined that he wasn't going to let his foot dictate everything in his life, but it did mean that he didn't walk up and down the stairs any more than necessary.

"Look," Tyler said after hugging him. "There are plenty of people, but it isn't packed."

"Maybe we—" Les was about to say that they should wait, but Tyler was already crossing the street, so he and Anthony followed.

The windows were adorable, showcasing classic children's books with some of the stuffed toys Dex must have found. He had turned one window into a reading garden with flowers, a few books, and a stuffed Ferdinand. The other had Clifford in it, romping through a window of undersized furniture, just like he did in the books. Les figured that the contents had to have been among Dex's mother's things. People on the street stopped to look. Some moved on; others went inside.

"Let's go see." Tyler bounded up the two steps to the door and pulled it open.

Inside, it felt like a party, with a few people browsing, a table of refreshments, and a group of children sitting around Dex as he read from Curious George in full-on actor mode, doing amazing voices. Jane manned the register, looking over the goings-on.

"The end," Dex said a few minutes after they walked in, and the six children clapped and got up, then let their parents guide them to the children's section.

"It looks like a success," Les said as Dex approached.

"Yeah, it's been pretty steady all day. I wanted to do something for the kids, so I planned the reading, and in half an hour, I have a few local authors coming in to read and sign their books," Dex said. Then he smiled and excused himself to help a few customers.

"In the past few days, Dex managed to arrange for a few deliveries from a couple of distributors, so he has some really fresh and hot titles," Jane explained. "Those are selling well. Sarah had already ordered some things, and those are out as well." She looked more cheerful than she had been the last time Les had seen her, but still, he could see the grief in her eyes. "I'm so proud of him for giving the store a try. It meant so much to Sarah, and this has breathed life back into it." She smiled, then turned away to help a customer.

"We're going to browse," Tyler said. He and Anthony wandered off, and Les looked around himself, thumbing through a few books and generally doing his best to stay out of the way. The pair of local authors—one wrote romance and the other thrillers—had set up their displays on a shared table. Before long, they were signing books and talking to customers, adding more energy to the evening.

"What's bothering you?" Tyler asked as he added another book to the stack Anthony was carrying.

"Nothing. This is wonderful." Les could sense the despondency he'd been feeling the past few months returning, and he had to push it away.

Dex came to stand next to him, and they shared a smile that helped make Les forget about his worries and his foot. He wanted to kiss him, but that wasn't a good idea. Still, Dex's eyes carried the invitation, and Les wanted to take him up on it… and more.

"Do you have game supplies?" a young man asked.

"I'm sorry," Dex answered, "I don't. But I believe there's a game store in Mechanicsburg that has a huge variety. If you join one of their clubs, it'll give you access to play all the games. I was researching things the store might carry and had stumbled on their website."

"Cool, thanks." The kid placed a book on the counter. Jane rang it up, and Dex excused himself to check on other customers.

"Has he stopped at all?" Les asked Jane.

She shook her head. "We opened at ten, and I could barely get him to take a break for lunch. He's talked to every customer, and he even created a suggestion box so people could tell him the kinds of things they want to see in the store." She sighed. "I think he's trying too hard." Then she turned back to the counter and answered a few questions.

Les slowly wandered the store and picked out a few books that he set aside. Dex brought him a chair, and Les sat down, feeling a little like a fool. He should have come closer to closing time. Now he felt like an old lady who needed a chair because he couldn't stand any longer.

"I'm glad you came." Dex put a hand on his shoulder, and just like that, the embarrassment vanished. "It's been a great day."

"That's good. People really seem to like what you've done."

"We've had some good publicity, and plenty of people have stopped in to say hello." He leaned down. "And I might have done enough business today that I can order some more new books and bring some additional items into the store." He seemed all smiles and full of energy, which Les found sexy as hell.

A little before eight, the last of the customers made their way out of the store. Tyler and Anthony talked to Dex and made their purchases before exchanging hugs. "You have fun."

"I'll behave myself," Les whispered.

"Don't you dare," Tyler told him as Anthony took their bag of books, and they left arm in arm out into the evening. Dex locked the door behind them with a smile.

LES WAITED while Dex and Jane closed up.

"That was a great day," Jane said as she began running the register to close up.

"I had hoped that there would be some excitement." Dex grinned and helped her get everything ready for the night. She left the register drawer open and locked the base money in the back while Dex made out a deposit slip, put it in a bank bag, and said good night to Jane.

"Thank you for everything today." Dex kissed her cheek, and she patted his shoulder. "I couldn't have done it without you."

"Sarah would be thrilled with all this. It's like the store used to be, years ago."

"I'm thinking of starting a book club and doing a children's reading hour each week. Mom used to do that when I was a kid, and I loved it. I think it was something she did especially for me." He tucked the bank deposit bag under his arm. "Do you want to join us for dinner?"

Jane shook her head. "I'm going back to the house to pour some wine, heat up something to eat, and then put my weary feet up and watch television. You young people have fun."

When she left the store, Dex turned out the lights. Then he and Les got ready to go too, with Dex locking the door behind them on their way out.

They walked down to the bank, dropped the bag in the night deposit box, and continued slowly down the sidewalk. "How about Italian?" Dex asked.

"Sounds great." They continued to the square and went down half a block to a new Italian restaurant. They got a table, and the server brought water and menus, then left them alone. "What looks good to you?" Les asked.

"I'm in the mood for a pizza," Dex asked.

They chose a large meat lover's and drinks. "I'm thrilled that the reopening went so great. Is it what you expected?"

Dex smiled. "It went better than I thought it would. I wasn't sure if anyone would show up. But we sold a lot of books, and I got some good suggestions about what people want. Maybe I can figure out a way to keep new stock coming in. I had to use Jane's credit card to buy the new stock I got for today, but I sold enough that I can pay her back and then some. Mom had the store, but there was never a lot of money, and what there was needed to go to Jane. So I'm sort of starting over in a way."

"I guess it's all about cash management."

"Yup. The authors sold some books, and I got a percentage, but I didn't take much. I wanted them to do well, and they were doing me a favor. The ladies said that they know more authors, so hopefully I can have more signings. Local authors usually bring in a few people." He was so hyped up. "Tomorrow I'm going to go through the suggestions and see if there's anything else that might help. Maybe place another book order."

"I can't tell you how happy I am that things went well." He probably should have told some of the guys he'd worked with about the opening. Maybe he'd send them a message tomorrow to help spread the word. "I like to think that this town rises to the occasion. Like this restaurant. This building has been eight places in as many years, but this looks great and…." The server took that opportunity to bring out their pizza, which smelled amazing and had Les's belly rumbling. "Don't give up and it will work out. People loved your mom."

"Yeah, they did. But that isn't going to sustain the store over the long haul. Tonight I pulled out all the stops. I can't do that every day."

"The biggest thing to do is carry what people want and be friendly—give customers something the big stores can't: personal service and a little conversation," Les offered. "Get to know your customers and they'll stick by you." He portioned out a slice for each of them and took a bite. "God, this is good." The sauce had a spicy bite that had him groaning deep in his throat.

"It is." Dex leaned forward. "Most food here skews way too sweet for me. Since I moved away, I've figured out that central Pennsylvania is the great American food desert, where gravy is a drink and sugar is a spice."

Les smiled. He had never thought about it because he was from the area and used to it, but Dex was right.

"Potato salad and macaroni salad are sweet, as is the coleslaw. Sometimes it's like candy."

"I suppose you're right."

"I didn't think anything about it before I left, but since I've come back…." He shivered a little. "A lot of things just don't taste right anymore. I know it's because I'm used to something else." Dex took another bite of his pizza, and Les watched him, eating slowly and getting lost in those intense eyes.

"Can I ask you something?" Les set down his slice.

"Sure," Dex responded. "As long as it isn't about books or the store. I've had enough of those questions for today."

Les swallowed hard. He hadn't been thinking along those lines at all, but now that Dex mentioned it, he was curious about whether Dex had found anything unusual when he'd searched through the storage areas to find things to complete his windows.

Les knew Tyler was probably right and he needed to let go of whatever suspicions he had. If Sarah had been boosting the store with some side business activity in order to keep it afloat, that had probably died with her. But then, maybe it hadn't. Dex didn't seem to know anything about it, but Les had no proof. It was all supposition. And if he simply let it go and relaxed a little, then he might be able to enjoy himself. Dex was a nice guy, and he seemed interested in him. Les needed to simply enjoy that and put the cop portion of his personality on hold. After all, his police career was clearly on ice anyway. Still, he kept coming back to the fact that if Sarah had been selling something illicit out of the store to keep it going, then maybe something about that could lead him back to the dealers who were responsible for putting him out of commission. And that alone drew him forward. His gut told him there had been something going on. He'd be a fool to ignore it.

There was another element to this as well. If Sarah had somehow been involved with the drug ring, and if Dex knew nothing about it, that could put Dex in danger. And that he couldn't allow.

"Where are you?" Dex queried lightly. "You were suddenly gone for a few seconds."

"Sorry," he said quietly as he tried to remember his question. "Oh yeah." He smiled. "When you were in LA, what did you do for fun? I know it's huge city and that they have everything…."

Dex chuckled. "I lived a real LA lifestyle. I used to work a lot, went to auditions. On hot days I went to the beach, which is more about being seen than going in the water. It's pretty cold a lot of the year because the currents come down from Alaska." He flashed a smile that made Les want to lean over the table and share it with him. "There's all kinds of tourist stuff, but like most people who live there, I rarely did any of it."

Les took a bite of his pizza. "And what did you do for fun when you lived here?"

Dex leaned farther over the table. "Finish your pizza and I'll show you," he whispered.

Les felt his eyes widen and he ate more quickly.

Once they had polished off the large pizza and their sodas, Dex paid the bill and they got ready to go. "Stay here. I'm going to hurry back to the house to get the car and I'll come pick you up." Dex held Les's hand over the table. "It won't take me very long." He flashed a wicked smile and then stood and hurried out the door.

Les watched out the front window for a few minutes, smiling to himself, before getting up and using the cane for balance to go down the stairs and step out into the night.

Cars passed on the main street, and Les leaned against the building to take some of the weight off his foot. Minutes later, Dex pulled up in what had to have been his mother's old light blue Toyota.

For some reason Les saw Dex in something sportier and more fun…
and definitely not that color.

"I turned in the rental a few days ago," Dex explained once Les
got himself inside and the door closed. Then Dex took off, heading
south out of town.

"Where are we going?"

"You asked me what I used to do for fun, so I'm going to
show you."

Les wondered what Dex had in mind. There wasn't a great deal
out to the south, just a few small towns and eventually the orchards of
Adams County. "But…."

"Don't worry." Dex made a turn off the main road, heading
west. Soon the road began to climb and grew steeper. "An old friend
and his family owned this when I was a kid. They still do, as far as I
know." They continued upward, with thick trees on both sides of the
road. Then suddenly they broke into the clear. The area must have
been logged at some point, because they continued upward a little
longer with no trees before Dex turned off and parked.

"You used to come up here?" Les asked.

"Yeah. My friends and I considered it our secret place. Usually
we just came up here to drink and sometimes smoke." Dex grinned
in the moonlight that shone through the windshield. "But I probably
shouldn't talk about that, should I, Officer?" Dex's eyes filled with
mischief.

"Asshole," Les teased right back. "Is that all you did up here?"
The view was spectacular, with the valley behind them dotted with
lights all the way back to Carlisle.

"No," Dex whispered and leaned over the seat. "We used to
come up here because it was quiet and no one else knew about this
place. We talked about all those things that are important to a kid at
that age." Dex's fingers slid under Les's chin, and Les turned toward
him just in time for Dex's lips to find his.

Les closed his eyes, letting the kiss wash over him. Dex's lips
were firm, yet he was still gentle, and when he shifted closer, he
deepened it without pressing his weight onto him. "I take it this was
your make-out spot."

"It was for the other kids I knew." Dex backed away slightly, holding Les's gaze. "I never had anyone to make out with—I wasn't out when I was in high school. Imagine this town twelve, fourteen years ago. It wasn't as accepting as it is now, and I just wasn't brave enough to step forward. I used to come up here to get away from Mom and Dad, then eventually, just Mom. This was where I used to talk to my dad once he was gone."

"And you brought me here?" Les asked.

"I probably gave up a little too much information." He closed the distance between them once again. "I brought you here because I never had anyone to make out with before."

Les swallowed hard. "You mean I'm the first guy you've ever brought up here?"

"Yeah. I've made out with guys before... and done plenty of other things. But I never brought someone up here before, and I had forgotten about the view. Though when I was in high school, that was the last thing on my mind."

"So you brought me here to make out?" Les asked, slipping his arms around Dex's neck. "I like how you think; now let's get with the making." Then he tugged him down and met Dex halfway. Their lips touched, and Les groaned softly.

Dex's hand slipped through his hair, cupping his head. Les tried to lean toward Dex, but his arm banged the console between them. Les barely noticed with the way Dex's lips tasted. He shifted in the seat to try to deepen the kiss, and the seat belt grabbed, pinning him in place, each movement making it tighter. Les popped off his seat belt for more maneuverability and somehow managed to knock his head on the rearview mirror. He sat back, and when Dex pressed closer, leaning over the console, the horn sounded. Both of them jumped, and Les managed to bonk Dex's head. This car didn't have a great deal of make-out room, apparently.

Dex sat back with a huff. "I guess things worked better when we were kids."

Les chuckled. "Or more desperate to get laid." He smiled and stroked Dex's cheek. "The idea was sweet and the view is spectacular... and not just the one outside the car. But...." He tried not to laugh as he rubbed where he'd bumped his head.

"I know." Dex joined him, rubbing his head as well.

Les opened his door and got out of the car. Dex did too, and once the light went out, Les leaned against the door with Dex standing in front of him.

"I think this will be a lot more comfortable."

Les agreed and pulled Dex close until their hips and chests pressed together. God, that felt good.

"Now I have just one more comment," Dex asked, his lips right next to Les's, his hot breath sliding over them.

"And what's that?"

"I think I can feel my desperation rising," Dex whispered.

Les snorted, completely undignified. "Is that what they're calling it now, or did you name yours that because of a long drought?"

"No. His name is Clarence, but he's getting desperate… and he's definitely rising." Dex ran his hands down Les's back until they cupped his butt. Les closed his eyes, relishing the touch. The truth was that he had come to doubt whether anyone would ever touch him again.

"Clarence?" Les kissed Dex and then pulled away. "You know, I'm not sure I can be with a guy who calls his dick Clarence. Woody maybe… even Sparky… I think I could even live with the Roman Candle of Love. But Clarence?" He tightened his hold, even as he teased.

"Are you making fun of my dick? You haven't even met him in person yet and you're already dissing him." Dex held him closer, with Clarence definitely making his sizable impression known. Dex took Les's lips, pressing him back against the door of the car, where Les could feel every curve of the metal against his back. Talk about being between a rock and a hard place… or a hard dick. But Les was thrilled, and the temperature around them rose by the second. The chirping of the crickets receded and his own soft moans filled the darkness. Even the sweetness that hung in the air was overpowered by Dex's intensely musky scent. It threatened to sweep away Les's last remnants of self-control. He pressed closer, needing more, and Dex gave it.

Then, suddenly, Les pulled away again, in need of air and a little distance. He swallowed hard, feeling the last of his resistance crumbling around him.

"Why did you stop?" Dex asked, not moving away.

"Because...." He paused. Was it so hard to admit that he was scared? That the idea of opening his heart again, only to have it smashed, scared the hell out of him? Les had lost so damned much already. He could live with not ever having someone like Dex in his life. But if he let him in and then lost everything again, he didn't know how he could keep himself from shattering into a million tiny pieces.

"You have to tell me. I can't read your mind," Dex told him softly.

"I know you're trying to make the store a success, and that must mean that you intend to stay here." Les felt as though he was trying to find the one safe path to walk in a sea of quicksand. His life had been like that since the accident, and he always thought that he was one wrong step from being swallowed up, never to return again.

"And there's a vacant apartment above the store. I'm going to have my things packed and shipped out here. There isn't all that much. But why are we talking about this at this particular moment?" Dex leaned forward again, his lips teasing at the base of Les's neck.

Les cradled Dex's head in his arm and stretched his neck to give him better access. "Because...." He groaned. "There's something important.... You said you can't read my mind, and...."

Dex huffed slightly. "I lied." He pulled away and met Les's gaze. "I can read exactly what you're thinking right now. I can feel it too. All this worry isn't going to get you anywhere."

"But it's you and this—between us—that I'm worried about." He finally broached the subject. "If this is something casual, something just for fun, between us, then...."

Dex stilled. "Of course being with you is fun. We even had a good time painting the store. Who would have thought painting with someone could be interesting? But it was. Don't you want to have fun?"

Les sighed. "I didn't mean it that way. I meant, basically, that you have me in your arms and I don't know what your intentions are." He snorted at his own words.

"I'd say that was pretty obvious. But if you want it spelled out...." Dex kissed him again. "I was thinking that you"—he slipped his hand under Les's shirt, slid it up his belly to his chest—"and I would get to know each other much better." Damn, Dex had a way of making Les's thoughts spin, and he forgot himself for a few seconds. One simple touch and Les was gone, his skin tingling and his mind already sprouting wings. He must be pathetically desperate, but he really didn't care. "I thought we'd go to your place, where I could get these clothes off you, and then see if my actor's imagination in any way lives up to glorious reality."

Les put his hand over Dex's to stop its roaming for a second. "That's what I need to know. Is this a one-night thing or… more?"

Dex nodded. "I don't know what it is, but I stopped one-night stands some time ago. I'm not looking just to have sex." Les nodded and released his hold on Dex's hand. "I got the idea that you weren't either."

"I'm not. But I'm…." Oh hell, he needed to let go of the desire for promises and assurances. No one could see the future. If Les wanted the chance at something possibly good, then he needed to take some risks.

"I think I know what you are. And we can take thing slow if that's what you need."

Les shook his head. "I just need to know that you aren't going to go running for the hills tomorrow."

Dex stiffened. "That guy who hurt you? I wish I could beat the crap out of him." He leaned over and whispered, "You know, I have never been violent, but I think that if you pointed him out to me, I'd grab him by the ears…" His voice was soft and enticing. "…lift him up, and pin him to a clothesline. Let him dangle in the breeze."

Les snickered. "There are so many things wrong with that statement… and you really need some help with your sexy talk. Now, maybe tie him to an anthill and cover him with honey. That would be cool. Well, mean but still cool." He'd have thought Dex's reference to Chad would be hard to deal with, but the way Dex casually wrote him off, as though he wasn't important other than in the way he'd hurt Les, somehow stripped the memory of some of its residual pain and power. It was something Les had been trying to figure out how to do for a long time, and Dex helped him do in a matter of minutes.

Dex sucked on his earlobe. "Maybe I should take you home and cover you with honey. I bet you're sweet enough. If the moans you're making are any indication, I'd say that you'd look, sound, and taste like something else."

Les held Dex's cheeks and kissed him hard. "Now that's the kind of sexy talk I could get behind."

Dex's hands slipped downward across his belly to Les's belt, two fingers sliding under the waistband and around to the front. "I can tell," Dex breathed. "Just stand still and don't move."

"Huh?" Les asked as his belt buckle clanked while Dex worked it open. Then the button on the front of his jeans snapped open, loosening the tension around his waist. "What are you doing?"

"Necking isn't the only reason I brought you up here." He teased the skin over the waistband of Les's boxers and…. Les stiffened in more ways than one. A zing of heat raced through him. Les clamped his eyes closed, willing Dex to continue. Hell, he wanted to be touched, to not feel like some sort of gimpy eunuch. Les put his hand on Dex's.

"What is it? Do you want me to stop?"

"God no." He caught his breath, sliding a hand around the back of Dex's neck. "It's…."

"Then what?" Dex purred into his ear.

"You really see me," Les said.

Dex stilled and backed away slightly. "Of course I see you. What's not to see? Or like?"

"No. I mean, you really see me. Maybe it's the cane, but sometimes I feel invisible. I'm a young guy who has trouble walking most of the time. But most people can't see past my limp. It's like I don't exist." Les sighed. "I don't mean that people really don't see me, but they don't think of me… you know…." He tugged Dex closer. "I'm supposed to be a nice person, happy, thrilled when people try to help me. But not sexual. At least, that's not what people expect."

Dex was right back, pressing to him, his hands at Les's waist, pushing his pants lower. "And you thought I didn't see you as a sex god? Because let me tell you, with those shoulders, that narrow waist, your intense gaze, and…." Dex slipped his hand into Les's boxers and around his cock. "Let's just say, the sex god has plenty of hidden assets."

Les whimpered as pleasure raced through him. "Dex, we're outside. I'm a cop...or at least I was...." Dex gripped him tighter, stroking slowly, and damned if Les could remember what he was going to say. "Dex...."

"What, is this really illegal?" Dex pressed closer, pushing Les against the car so he couldn't get away. Not that he wanted to. The friction was delicious, and he wanted everything Dex could give him. "Come on. There's no one around and we're on the top of the world up here. It's dark, we can't be seen, and I have you all to myself."

Les's leg bounced with the increase in pleasure, and he wasn't sure how much longer he was going to be able to hold off... or how he could stay upright. His foot throbbed in time with the blood to his cock, and it only added to the pleasure of the moment. "Of course it's illegal to have sex in public where we could be seen." He groaned softly and clamped his eyes closed.

"But this isn't public. There's no one around to see or hear anything. Our only witnesses are the stars." Dex sucked on his ear once again. "Let me give the stars something to see." He tugged Les's cock out and stroked harder. "That's it. Just go with it. Let everything else go and look up. The stars are watching, seeing how sexy you are. They don't care about your foot. They shine down on you and me regardless of anything else." He sucked harder, and Les pulled away just enough so he could turn his head and kiss him.

"Dex... I...."

"Just let go. No one can hear, so yell your pleasure to the skies."

Les lifted his gaze. There were millions of stars, and as he watched, they seemed to get closer and closer.

"That's it," Dex whispered as tingles began at the base of Les's spine, making him shiver.

Les bit his lip as the intensity built, and before he knew it, it seemed as if the stars were spinning all around him. "Dex!" Les closed his eyes as his knees threatened to buckle from under him. He leaned back against the car, using it to keep himself upright as he inhaled deeply, desperate to get air into his lungs. "What did you do to me?" Whatever it was, Les was breathless, yet felt more alive than he had in a while.

"Can you stand?"

Les managed to nod. It took a few seconds before the world seemed right again, and when it did, he saw the concern in Dex's eyes. Les tugged Dex near and kissed him hard, determined to give Dex everything that he'd just been gifted. Damn, it felt good to be on his feet once again, with Dex melting against him. It seemed to Les that he might have found some of his inner strength again. His injury was what it was, but Les had let it define him. That needed to come to an end.

"I'm okay." God, he was so much better than okay. His heart raced and his chest filled with the night air. He grasped Dex was all his strength, determined to hold the man the way he deserved to be held. Les pulled Dex down into another kiss, working open Dex's belt as something flashed around him.

It took Les a second to realize that the lights weren't in his imagination. Someone was coming up the hill, and he still had his dick out. Somehow he managed to get himself back into his pants, and Dex pulled open the car door. They both got in, started the car, and pulled out. They began the trek down and passed another car just as the crest disappeared behind them. "Do you have a thing with sex outdoors? Because it seems I have a thing for sex outdoors with you."

Dex chuckled as he continued down the mountain, the headlights cutting the darkness. "I guess you could say that. I love to be outdoors. I used to hike and camp on the beach in parts of California with some friends, and it always—"

"Made you horny?" Les asked.

"Yeah." He chuckled softly. "But I was never able to do anything about it. I didn't really hide my sexuality when I was in California, but I wasn't out marching in Pride parades either. There is still some apprehension around gay actors in Hollywood. No matter how many stars have come out, very few of them were out and became famous. Most became very successful and then came out."

As they reached the bottom of the hill and continued back toward town, Les settled into his seat, content and surprisingly happy. "I suppose."

"So now that I'm home again, I get to be myself," Dex admitted. "In a lot of ways, the pressure is off. I know my mom cared for me, and I know that Jane does too. She's told me that I'm like the son she never got to have."

"Do you think she wanted children?" Les asked.

"I know she did. But it never worked out, and I hurt her pretty badly early on because I didn't want another mother. My dad was gone, and Mom was moving on. I resented both of them, but I think I took it out on Jane the most. But that was years ago, and she's forgiven me for being such a pain in the ass. She, Mom, and I were a family. So I'm her family now. But she told me once that she always wished she had been able to have a child of her own." Dex paused. "I don't know if that means she never got the chance or she just wasn't able." He pulled to a stop at a light outside town.

"Have you ever thought of having kids?" Les asked. "A lot of the younger guys on the force do, and I feel a little jealous of them." He was being honest. "I always saw myself as having a family."

Dex pulled through the intersection once the light changed. "I guess I never considered it. I was an only child because Mom lost two other babies. I was her third try, and after that, I guess I was enough for her so she stopped trying. I didn't spend a lot of time around babies because there weren't many of them around. I didn't have cousins who had babies. A few of my mother's friends had smaller kids, but I wasn't around them much." His body seemed to tense a little, and then he relaxed again. "I have to admit, babies scare me a bit—they're so helpless. But I suppose having one of my own would be different."

"My cousins had lots of kids, so I'm used to them." He smiled. "I love babies and they love me. My sister, Maria—she's in North Carolina now, and her husband is in the service—I used to put their son, Ethan, to bed because I was the only one able to get him to sleep." He rested his hand on Dex's leg and let the subject drop. It seemed uncomfortable for Dex, and Les didn't want to mess things up. It wasn't like having kids was a deal-breaker or anything.

Les gave Dex directions around to the back of his building where he could park, and they went in together. "Do you need any of the stuff in the back seat?" he asked as he got out.

"No." Dex peered back into the back, reaching for an old paperback with a creased spine. He closed it quickly, but not before

Les noticed that it seemed to have been hollowed out. Dex set it back on the seat. "It's just some stuff from the store that I meant to take into the house." He closed the door, and Les did the same. "Mom kept some interesting things at the store."

Les chuckled. "I bet she did." He hoped he sounded natural. Whatever was going on there, Les was pretty certain Dex didn't know about it. But that didn't mean he didn't need to be protected, in case it posed a threat.

Chapter 6

DEX FOLLOWED as Les slowly climbed the stairs along the side of the building. They were steep and rather narrow. "I don't usually come this way. The front stairs are easier, but this is more convenient." At the top, Les unlocked the front apartment door and walked in, gesturing for Dex to follow him.

"Are you okay?" Dex asked as he passed. "You're all tense." He stepped inside and pulled Les to him as soon as he closed the door. "We don't have to do anything that you aren't comfortable with. There's no requirement that we need to do anything."

Les seemed really stiff, and his anxiety seemed to be building. Dex didn't understand it. Les had been so relaxed most of the way home. Maybe it was the talk about kids.

Finally Les seemed to shake it off. "I'm better than okay. I really am." The curtains were closed, and Les guided Dex toward the sofa. "Do you want anything to drink? I have some beer and a bottle of wine, a few sodas, stuff like that."

"Whatever you're having," Dex said. "Do you want me to help get it?"

"It's okay." Les went to the kitchen, leaning on his cane, and Dex rolled his eyes. Of course Les was tense. He was probably hurting. When he returned with two beers, Dex made room for him on the sofa.

"Does massage help your foot?" Dex guided Les back until his feet rested on his lap. Dex gently took off Les's shoes and socks, then softly rubbed the skin of his scarred foot and ankle. The lines were still a little pink but were starting to fade. He made sure to make no quick movements.

Les leaned back on the pillows. "God, that's feels good," he sighed, then tensed again. He probably hated feeling this way and was afraid of looking weak.

"Did I hurt you?" Dex asked, stopping instantly.

"No. It's just that other than the doctor, I don't let people see my feet. I mean, they aren't pretty...."

"There's nothing to be ashamed of or squeamish about. They're feet. I have the ugliest feet ever. Awful feet run in my family. I hate to say it, but when we took car rides as a family, I had the back seat to myself, and I used to like to get comfortable."

"So you'd take your shoes off," Les supplied.

"Yup. After two minutes my parents would be yelling at me to put my shoes on. They said I was clouding up the back window."

Les sighed and closed his eyes. "So you're Mr. Stinky Feet?"

"I used to be. I was one of those kids who was always active, and I had a lot of foot trouble growing up. Still do. They get dry and stuff.... God, this is the dumbest conversation. Feet. There has to be something more interesting to talk about." He continued lightly rubbing Les's foot, even as he leaned over him. "Maybe we could talk about what we did earlier."

"You mean your public sex fetish?" Les smirked.

"Are you complaining? I certainly didn't hear objections when you were yelling across the mountain at the top of your lungs." He ran his hand up Les's leg toward his knee, loving the way he shivered under his touch.

"Dex, you're really naughty."

"Maybe. But again, I don't hear you complaining. Though I can tell that something is turning you on."

Les moaned softly, and Dex slid his hand back to Les's foot. He took a drink of his beer, watching Les as he did the same. He wished he was in the right position to kiss that spot on this throat that worked just right as he swallowed. Damn, something about Les really got him going.

"Are you getting tired?" Dex asked.

"Not really, but that doesn't mean that we can't go to bed." The sparkle in Les's eyes was mischief personified. "Maybe you could rub my foot again...."

Dex snorted. "And other things as well." He was more than ready to be able to explore all of Les.

Dex finished his beer, and Les did the same. Then Dex waited for him to get to his feet. He thought of offering to help, but refrained—

Les was proud. So he waited patiently, then followed him to the bedroom, turning out the lights as they went.

"What I want to know is how you managed to get that up here." The room was really large, and the bed was gorgeous—king-sized, with a rich deep green coverlet that accentuated the light gray walls.

"Some of my friends gave me a hand," Les said, sitting on the end. "I like to spread out when I sleep, and…." He lowered his gaze. Dex got the idea that the bed might have been purchased just before the accident with someone else in mind.

"It looks amazing." He sat next to Les and took his hand. "Whatever you want." This had to be nerve-racking.

Les set his cane aside and scooted back on the bed, lying with his head on the pillows. "There were so many times when I thought that a bed this big was just stupid and that I should get rid of it for something more practical and less…."

"Huge?" Dex teased. Not that he was at all disappointed.

"I was going to say lonely. But huge works too."

Dex took off his shoes and lay back next to Les. His choice of words was telling.

"I really hate that…." He sighed and grew quiet. Dex let Les finish what he wanted to say. "I used to wonder what I'd be if I wasn't a cop, and even after all these months, I can't come up with anything. It was all I ever wanted to be when I was a kid, and I got to do it. Now I can't, so I've been trying to think of something else. I can't just sit home for the rest of my life. I won't."

Dex could understand that. "Close your eyes," he said softly. "You say you can't be a police officer. So take that off the table and imagine yourself as something else. We used to do exercises like this in some of my acting classes. We had to be different professions and take various roles. You can't play the cop any longer, so picture yourself as something else."

Les lay still and groaned. "Like what? I could be Gimpy, the private detective, except I'd stick out like a sore thumb."

"Just relax…." He gently rubbed Les's arm. "Let your mind empty. You're in a safe place. You don't have to be on guard. I'm right here with you, and nothing is going to happen. So let yourself just float."

Les smiled. "I used to want to be a rock star, except I'm tone deaf."

"You're also a great kisser. Maybe you could parlay that into a new career."

Les snorted. "Yup. I could be a rent boy for people with a cane fetish."

Dex chuckled softly. "Just close your eyes and relax. This is supposed to be visualization exercise, and I don't want to be thinking of you on a street corner, waving your cane provocatively at cars, asking guys if they're interested in a date." He rolled his eyes as Les laughed, his shoulders sagging. "Okay, let's try again. Relax and close your eyes."

"I can't do this. All I see myself doing is standing on a street corner in a belly shirt and tight jeans, leaning on my cane, looking a lot like Grandpa Simpson."

Dex lost it, falling back onto the pillow, laughing as he looked up at the ceiling. "I was trying to help you."

"Yeah, I know. But you were the one who suggested I try to make a career out of kissing, for cripes sake." They both chuckled, and then they grew quiet.

Dex realized that some acting exercise wasn't going to help Les figure out the direction he wanted to take in his life in ten minutes or less. That was probably dumb. Les needed to work through that himself. "I wish I could help you."

Les sighed. "I'm thinking that I need to help myself. I thought of going back to school. Maybe I could become an accountant or something."

Dex doubted that was the answer. "What you understand is law enforcement. You did that for a couple of years. So look at other things in that area. You could probably teach or something. There has to be another career path."

Les shrugged. "I'd like to teach, but I don't have enough years on the force for that. If I'd been more senior and had had a chance to move up the ranks, I might have had a chance." He paused. "I had considered doing behind-the-scenes work on investigations."

"How about security? Have you done any work with cybercrimes and that sort of thing? I bet there's a lot of opportunity there." Dex really did want to help, but he was drawing a blank. He rolled onto his side. "I guess you could say I'm out of ideas."

"It's okay. I haven't had any myself, and I've been searching for something for months." Les rolled to face him. "I'll figure it out eventually. I have to get my mind around the fact that there's more to me than just my foot."

Dex took Les's hand and gently swirled his thumb over Les's palm. Slowly, he closed the distance between them. Les met him partway, and Dex gathered Les closer and rolled them so Les's weight pressed him into the mattress. Dex wanted Les to have as much freedom of movement as possible, and damn, it was exciting. Despite Les's injured foot, he was solid and strong. There were few things as sexy as having a strong man press him into the mattress.

"Is this okay?" Les asked.

Dex smiled. "Honey, this is damned near perfection." He held Les tighter, spreading his legs and winding them around Les's waist. The man was sexy, that was for sure, with thick arms and all that muscle. Dex slid his hands down Les's back and tugged up his shirt until Les pulled away and Dex could get his shirt off. Damn, Les was luscious. Dex wanted all of him but didn't know where to start.

Les's muscles were solid under his hand as he pressed it to his chest. "You're something else."

"Not too heavy?" Les asked.

Dex tilted his head to the side. "God no." He wanted to climb Les like a fucking sex tree. "Why would you think that?" He smoothed over Les's cheeks. "Did Chad say something to you?"

Les nodded. "He was always afraid that I was going to squish him. Chad was willowy and lithe. He could dance like nobody's business, but he was definitely smaller."

"Well, I'm not going to break." Dex wound his arms around Les's neck. "So why don't you shimmy out of those pants and let me get mine off, and then you and I can see just how athletic you want to make things." Dex loved a man who wasn't afraid to use a little strength.

"I'm not sure...."

"Just be yourself," Dex told him.

Les slid off the bed and took off his shoes and pants. Dex didn't waste any time either, getting undressed and bouncing on the mattress. "Yeah… now that's a view." Les had an incredible ass, round and tight enough to bounce nickels off of. Dex loved a man with a great ass, and this one was picture perfect. He told himself he wasn't going to drool as Les slowly turned around. He was stunning in all his naked glory. Dex's mouth went dry.

"You can say that again." Les looked him over with a penetrating gaze that almost felt as though Les was running his hands over him. Intense didn't begin to describe it.

"Come get back on the bed." Dex slid over as Les crawled back onto the mattress. They were both hard, and Dex's cock throbbed as Les got closer. He had wanted to know what Les kept hidden under his clothes, and now all that glorious golden-tan skin was on full display. Dex was determined to take in as much of him as possible. Drawing Les closer, he kissed him, guiding Les down on top of him, chest to chest, hips to hips. He groaned as Les pressed into him. The air-conditioned room did nothing to cool the heat that flared between them in moments. "Damn.…"

"You like what you see?"

"Yes." He smoothed down Les's back and over the small above the curve of his hard ass, gripping the cheeks and groaning softly in Les's ear. "You are one hell of a package, and boy am I glad it's all unwrapped." He felt like this was the best Christmas morning ever.

Les chuckled. "You're not so bad yourself. You must have worked out a lot."

"I wanted to be an actor in Hollywood, the shallowest place on earth. It was all about how you looked or who you knew. I did my best to always look as good as possible. So yeah, a couple hours a day at the gym wasn't out of line." He tugged Les down into a kiss. This wasn't the time for words but for a very different kind of communication, one that involved every part of their bodies, with their lips put to a much hotter and more tantalizing use.

Dex loved the taste, the tangy saltiness of Les's chest right around the nipple. When Dex closed his lips around the bud, Les moaned softly, but with a rumble from deep in his throat that only built Dex's own desire. Les's smooth skin flowed under his hands as he roamed his strong body, wanting more. Dex's lips followed his outstretched fingers, hands, mouth, eyes all feasting on Les for as long as possible. Each muscular curve and enticing divot drew him forward. He wanted everything all at once, as if Les was a feast and he was a starving man.

Dex liked to think he understood men—he was one, after all, and he slept with them. He knew what he liked, so he explored a little to see where their pleasures met up, and to his surprise, they seemed to match up just fine. Each moan he elicited was accompanied by an equal exploration and a zip of pleasure with an echo that returned to him. Back and forth, ebbing and flowing, they took their time. Dex loved that neither of them seemed to be in a huge hurry. Small touches and nipped tastes built and became firmer, more intense and demanding.

"Dex?" Les asked, his gaze pleading, and Dex nodded. Les then reached to the bedside table and pulled out the supplies they needed.

"I want that," Dex whispered into the shadowed room, stroking his hands over Les's cheek and then down to his rolling cannonball shoulders. The man was stunning, and the more he explored, the more he loved what he found. There was a strength in Les that he likely didn't even realize was there. Dex felt it, and it wasn't the rippling muscles but an internal rod of steel that might have become a little bent because of Les's trials, but it was still there. "How do you want me? What will be easier?"

Les didn't hesitate. "Just like this. I want to be able to see you." Les was firm but slow and caring, preparing him with enticing movements that crossed Dex's eyes more than once and left him ready and aching for more. Les seemed to know how to touch and give, yet he never gave quite enough… never all… leaving Dex on the edge, willing and wishing for more.

Even as Les filled him, their gazes joining, it wasn't enough—until it was. Until Les decided it was, and then Dex held on to him tightly and went along with the bed-shaking ride that he hoped never came to a stop.

Nothing was ever perfect, and Dex didn't expect it to be. Sex was messy, sloppy, and sometimes fumbling. This was all that, with so much more on top that the imperfections became barely noticeable because of the energy, drive, the electric passion that Les generated that engulfed them, took over. Worlds passed through Les's eyes, freely given yet delivered with energy and enough energy to power a city, and Dex took and offered them right back.

Dex had expected Les to be less forceful, but he was more like banked power, always on the edge but keeping it in check, which was sexy as fuck. Les let him see and feel his power, but not the full brunt of it, making him want more. "You don't need to treat me like I'm made of glass," Dex argued.

"Well… I…," Les said.

Dex tugged him down. "I mean it. I'm not what's-his-face. You aren't going to hurt me, and I like things a little powerful. Your strength is a turn-on, so don't hide it. Just be yourself, not some quiet version of yourself that you think you have to be to please someone who isn't here." Then Dex kissed him harder, deeper, stoking Les's flame, and sure as hell, the fire burst to life in both Les's body and his eyes.

Oh, he was still careful, but much more intense. Sweat broke out on his chest, which glistened in the light that shone around the curtains. Dex held on tight as Les took him on a rocket ride to the moon and beyond until the entire world broke into stars of pleasure and Dex fell back to earth, only to land in Les's arms and in his bed, surrounded by warmth.

"WHERE ARE you going?" Les asked the following morning as Dex tried to get out of bed without waking him.

"I need to get to the store. I figured that after last night, you'd need your rest." He leaned over the bed to give Les a kiss. "I also need to get home to shower and change before I go in." He expected he was going to get questions from Jane, and he didn't need any repeat customers speculating why he was wearing the same clothes. "I'm sure you have things to do. The store closes at six tonight."

"Maybe dinner?" Les asked. "Or is that too much? I don't want you to get sick of me."

"No, it's great. I'll call you when I close the store, and we can meet somewhere." He shared another kiss with Les. Then he dressed and left down the back stairs to his car.

His body ached in places he hadn't in a while, and by the time he got to the house, Jane had already left. Dex showered and changed his clothes before going in to the store. He pulled the remaining stock from the back, verified prices, and shelved it. Then, since he had a little time before the store opened, Dex pulled out some boxes his mother had in the back and carried them to the counter to go through.

"Well, I'll be…." The first box contained more books. He put them on the shelves and opened the next one. This one contained various paperbacks. He carried the box to the romance shelves and began stocking them. One of the books fell from his fingers and dropped to the floor. A small bag popped out. "What the hell?" He picked up the book and the bag.

It wasn't hard to discern what was inside. As soon as he opened the bag, the sweet scent he remembered from college and a few parties in LA told him exactly what it was. Dex closed the bag and slipped it back inside the hollow book, then went through the shelf to retrieve the other books he'd just put out. Each was hollow and filled with a similar bag.

"Holy shit," he said under his breath as the realization washed over him. Now he knew what those other hollow books were for, and he thought he understood how his mother had kept the store going.

He almost dropped the box at the knock on the front door. Dex glanced up to see Les smiling through the glass. He nearly tripped over his own feet rushing to put the box of hollow books back behind the counter before he went to open the door.

"I thought you might be hungry." Les stepped inside and handed him a paper bag. "I made egg sandwiches with ham for breakfast and brought you one." He kissed Dex and then turned back toward the door. "I hope you have a great day and sell out the store." Then he left, and Dex leaned against the checkout counter, wondering what he was going to do.

He could just flush the pot down the toilet and be done with it. That would probably be the smartest thing to do, especially since the guy he was seeing had been a police officer. But hell, what if his mother owed someone for the stuff? If that was the case, maybe he could give it back and that could be the end of it. He picked up the box and took it to the back room, where he tried to find a place to hide it and keep anyone else from stumbling onto it. In the end, Dex slipped the box into a black plastic garbage bag and wrapped the ends around it before placing the box on a bottom shelf just above the floor, all the way back and out of sight.

Now all he had to do was figure out what to do with the knowledge that his mother had been a pot pusher.

It was nearly nine, so he washed his hands and up his arms, just in case. Then he dried off, unlocked the front door, and flipped the sign to Open, hoping he had some customers.

BUSINESS WASN'T going like gangbusters, but it was steady. A lot of people wanted to talk about his mother, and Dex couldn't help wondering which, if any of them, had been aware of her little side business. He found himself looking differently at everyone, especially the young, hip couple who came in and went right for the more erotic books on the shelf near the counter. He even looked at the old men, wondering if they were coming in because his mother had been the one bringing a little extra joy to their lives. He tried to imagine his mother explaining to a customer that she had "some really good shit" this week.

Dex shook his head. He needed to keep his mind on his task rather than wondering about each person who came through the door. But he kept going back to that box under the shelves in the back room. What the hell was he going to do with it? There had to be enough product in those books to send him to jail for quite some time, and now his fingerprints were all over it. The thing was, he didn't know what to do about it or who to ask. Les was out of the question—he was a cop. And Dex didn't know that many people in town. The ones he trusted enough to ask were out of state. But hell, he didn't want to talk about this shit over the phone.

Jane might know something about it, though he was afraid to ask. If she did, he'd have thought she'd have mentioned something earlier. Either that, or she'd have gotten the goods out of the store. "Damn it, Mom," he muttered.

"What, young man?" an elderly customer asked as she approached the counter. She was using a cane and walked hunched forward.

"Sorry, I was just thinking out loud. How can I help you?" He smiled.

The lady leaned a little closer to the counter. "Those cards are so beautiful. My sister reads Tarot, and I bet she'd love those." The smile on her lips remained for a few seconds, and then her face tightened for a few seconds, as if she was in pain, before relaxing again.

"Are you okay?" Dex asked.

She nodded slowly. "I'm looking for some books on homeopathic medicine," she explained. "Your mother used to have quite a collection, and I'm trying to find some natural pain relief." She smiled. "You look a lot like her. Sarah was a dear heart, and there are so many of us in town who are going to miss her."

He swallowed. It warmed his heart that his mother was so loved. "I'm not sure I have anything." Dex stepped out from behind the counter. "There's just a small section of self-help and medical guides." He went over and looked at the shelves. "I'm sorry. I don't think there is anything like that here at the moment. I can look in the catalog and see about ordering a book for you. If you'd like to sit down, I can check what's available." He had determined that he was going to do his best to help each and every customer.

"I see," she said disappointedly. "Thank you, young man." She turned and slowly walked toward the door. Dex was a little concerned that she wasn't going to make it. Each step seemed like an effort for her. Dex hurried over to open the door.

"Please come back again... and I'll order any books you think you need." He waited until she was away from the store, waved, and then closed the door once more. He checked for other customers before picking up a duster and figuring that while it was slow, he'd clean up the place a little.

"How is business?" Les asked as he approached the counter later that afternoon. "I came to order a few books I wanted." He leaned a little on the counter, and Dex wondered if his foot might be bothering him. "I made a list." He passed it over. "I figured that since I'm going to have plenty of time, I might as well catch up on some reading."

"Of course." Dex happily got on the computer and placed an order for Les along with some other books he wanted to offer in the store. "How is your day going?"

"It's okay. I did some chores around the house and watched enough of the idiot box to turn my brain to mush. Do you have any idea how many home decorating competitions, cooking contests, and even flower arranging shows there are? It's enough to drive you up a tree. And the worst part is that they're all designed to be completely inane and ridiculous. They ensure that the most outrageous contestant wins and the best get tripped up on some technicality." He shook his head. "Maybe I should go on one about canes. Show people a million ways to use one for self-defense. Cane Slayer!" He brandished the metal cane like a sword.

Dex chuckled. "You're a goof. And yes, I know all about ridiculous television. I was even on some of those shows at one time or another. But somehow I can't see a program where you show people how to beat the crap out of each other with a cane. Though I'd love to see you on television."

The bell on the door tinkled and a group of ladies entered the store, talking among themselves.

"Can I help you ladies?"

"I hope so. Do you have any books on homeopathic medicine?" one of the older women asked.

Dex swallowed. "I'm sorry. I've had other people interested in that subject today. I'll be happy to order any books you need, but I don't seem to have any in the store." He looked at the silver-haired woman as her expression shifted from confusion to disappointment.

"I see. Well, thank you." She turned to leave, with the others following behind her.

"Have a good day, ladies," Dex called, more than a little perplexed.

"Yes. You too, young man," another of the ladies said. "All of us really loved your mother. She helped each and every one of us, and we're really going to miss her." They exited the store, leaving Dex wondering what the heck was going on.

"Maybe you should order some books on homeopathic medicine. Sounds like there's a real market for them," Les suggested. Dex nodded as a few more customers came in. "I'll see you after you close." Les squeezed his hand and then slowly walked toward the door, waving before he left the store.

BY CLOSING time, Dex had gotten two more requests for self-help books, and he wondered what the heck he should bring into the store to satisfy the demand. He locked the doors and took care of the day's takings. He was pleased and figured he'd take part of the day on Sunday to draw up a budget and maybe determine what stock he could buy for replenishment. It wasn't like he was going to bring in the same titles that had already sold. He needed new things to entice his customers.

"Half the town seems to want books on home remedies," Dex told Les as he was finishing up the closing process. "The other half seem to have browsed the store, and quite a few people bought books. It's been really great."

"That's wonderful," Les said with a smile.

"Now I just have to figure out how to keep the excitement going." He sighed, because excitement was the last thing he felt. Dex had been on all day, and his energy levels were wearing down. "I'm very worried that if I lose their interest, I'll never get it back. I don't want the store to get tired. There always needs to be something new." His head spun. Dex had never thought of himself as a merchant. Running a store had never been one of his dreams. When he was a kid, he had played with stages and acted out little stories that he either read or wrote. Pretend time was his favorite part of the day. But playing store? He'd never done that. And now he found himself in the role of shopkeeper for real.

Les drew him into a hug. "Just be yourself. You have this aura around you, a stage presence. So make it part of the store."

Dex sighed and hugged Les back. Holding him felt good. "You're saying I should perform?"

"No. I'm saying you should just be the bright, fun-loving person you are. Let that shine through and people will respond to it. As for the books people are requesting, I'd say you should try to accommodate what they're asking for. Did anyone place orders?"

Dex shook his head. "That was the part that confused me."

"Okay. Well, sometimes it's easy to ask for something. Maybe they wanted to look something up and not buy. That's always possible. Why don't you check the library? They might have those kinds of reference books. At least you could let your customers know where they can find the information they want." Les was trying to be helpful, but it had been one long day filled with surprises. When Dex sighed, Les released him and stepped back. "Did you want to come to my place? I was going to cook a little dinner."

Dex sighed again. "I'd love to, but Jane called half an hour ago and asked if I was coming home after I closed the store. I think she's really at loose ends." He bit his lower lip.

"Then you should spend some time with her," Les said. "I fully understand. She's lost and alone."

Dex nodded. "Mom passed so suddenly…. I think we're both still trying to get our minds around the fact that she's gone." He sent a message to Jane telling her he was on his way home, but she responded quickly that she was going eat and go to bed.

Les and I were thinking about getting some dinner, he texted. Would you like to come with us?

Dots appeared to indicate that she was responding. There is so much food here. More than I can possibly eat.

Dex got the message. He showed Les the text. "What about if we went over there? Do you mind? You don't have to come if you don't want." Dex really hated to leave Jane alone all the time.

"Of course not. I'll get a bottle of wine or something and meet you at the house," Les offered.

Dex saw Les to the door and finished up, wondering how he'd been lucky enough to have found someone as understanding as Les. His mind also went to that damned box. If Les found out what was in it, everything would be over. Les was a cop—and he'd always be one. He had even told Dex that on more than one occasion. So something illegal, like the amount of pot his mother had been selling and seemed to have on hand, without any of the proper licenses, was not going to go over with Les at all.

Dex was just about to turn off the lights when someone knocked on the front door. It was the woman from much earlier in the day. He unlocked the door, and she gingerly entered the store. "How can I help you?" he asked. "I'm just closing up."

She leaned on her cane and didn't speak until Dex had closed the door once more. "I know, but…." Her hand shook, and her eyes were filled with pain. "Your mother was a special lady, and she did a lot for other people." She met his gaze. "I'm going to miss her very much."

"Would you like to sit down?"

"No. Thank you," she said, still leaning in the cane. "This isn't easy for me to say, but your mother helped a lot of us." She swallowed and her hand shook even more. "Young man, I'm eighty-four years old, and at this point in my life, my body has decided to turn on me. My life is about managing the pain. It never ends. Your mother used to help me with that. Well, me and others."

"How did she do that?" Dex asked.

"This state is backward in many ways. One of them is in the treatment of pain." She set her purse on one of the shelves. "My doctor is an old fuddy-duddy, but he does what he can. I've asked for his help, but he doesn't believe in anything that might be new, the old fart."

"Why don't you stop beating around the bush and tell me what it is you really want to say," Dex prompted.

"Ah, yes, a bottom-line kind of man. My husband was one of those too. There is one thing that helps with the pain—marijuana. But I can't get it for medical use because my doctor doesn't believe in it."

Dex stifled his gasp. "Did you get it from my mother?"

She nodded. "Your mom had an arrangement with a young man from outside town to supply the product. When I came in and you didn't seem to understand what I was asking for, I realized you didn't know. And I assume that she was helping others as well."

Dex held his tongue. He wasn't ready to tell anyone about what he had found. "I see." He watched her watching him.

"I may be an old lady, and I know I don't look like much, but I can read people, and I have a feeling that you found something." She released her breath very slowly. "Sarah was a good lady." She shifted the cane slightly. "I'm taking a chance telling you any of this, but I used to get marijuana from her. As far as I know, your mother never used it. But she understood about the pain relief that it provides. It's one of the few things that allows me to function and remain active.

My arthritis is so bad that there are times when it hurts to breathe. Standing like this and walking, even with the cane, is sometimes an exercise in how much pain I can tolerate." Dex could almost feel the pain that flooded her eyes, and it was all he could do not to take a step back from it.

"Can't you get medical marijuana here in the state?" Dex asked. "I know in California, where I came from, there are dispensaries, and it's pretty easy to get a number of products in various forms."

She shook her head. "I finally managed to get a card and a prescription, but I can't just go to a pharmacy to get it. The process is very difficult because while the state legalized it, the federal government hasn't. And the state only grudgingly allows it, with more red tape to jump over than you can imagine…. And young man, my jumping days are long past." Her energy seemed to be waning. "I'm sorry to have bothered you with my troubles."

Dex didn't know what to say. Part of him was tempted to give her some of what was in back, but what if she happened to be the grandmother of a police officer who was trying to bust him? This sort of thing was way outside his comfort zone. He was in no way interested in being the pot supplier to little old ladies. But another part of him wanted to help. He was his mother's son, after all. "Let me guess: asking for a book on homeopathic medicine was the password."

"I'm afraid so, yes. Your mother came up with that. I don't know how clever it is, but now you know." She stared at him expectantly as if she wanted him to give up all his secrets. "I should go. I'm sorry if I shocked you or injured the memory of your mother. She was an amazing woman, and everything she did was only to help people. And if she made a little extra money on the side… well, she was the one taking the risks." She turned slowly toward the door. "What your mom did was a blessing."

Dex opened the door and helped her out of the store. Then she slowly headed down the sidewalk. He locked the door and gathered his things before switching off the light and heading out into the night, hurrying toward his mother's house.

He needed to think of it as Jane's house now. Dex had to get his things shipped from California and get furniture so he could move in

above the store. How he was going to find the money to do all that, he
wasn't sure, but he was going to have to make it happen. He'd figure
it out.

"I was wondering if something happened to you," Jane said once
he stepped inside. "Les has been here for ten minutes." She hugged
him. "He's in the sunroom in back. I have some things heating up, and
I thought we could eat out there. It's a nice evening with a wonderful
breeze."

"Sounds good. I got delayed by a customer." He stopped her
before she could go back to the kitchen. "How are you holding up? Is
everything okay?" He knew those were stupid questions—of course
things weren't okay.

"As well as they can be. I miss Sarah all the time. But it's the
nights that are hardest. During the day I can keep busy, but when
it's quiet at night, there's nothing to distract me from my thoughts."
He took her hand. "It's like I've got a hole in my heart and there's
nothing I can do to fix it. My friends tell me that it will get easier in
time.... They're probably right. But for now, it sucks." She went to
the kitchen.

Dex found Les sitting in one of the large chairs in the sunroom
at the back of the house, with his foot up on an ottoman. "Don't get
up." He leaned over the chair to kiss Les lightly, then sat down close
to him. "I'm sorry I'm late. I had a last-minute visitor who wanted to
talk a little about Mom, and I just didn't think I could cut her off." He
hated lying by omission to Les, but he didn't know how he'd react
to finding out that some of the little old ladies in town were buying
pot from his mother. What if that wasn't all she'd been selling? This
entire situation had him unsettled, but he could deal with that later.
Definitely not tonight.

"How was business?"

"Not bad. It's Saturday, so there were a number of families
walking around downtown. The kids seem to really like the windows.
I can see them through the glass, grinning, with wide eyes." He
smiled.

"I saw some folks outside the store this morning. It was an older
couple who told me how much they'd enjoyed reading stories to

their grandkids. I think the windows are a real hit. It's making people remember what it was like when things were simpler."

"Yeah. Now I have to keep it going, but I don't know how. Not really. I can bring in the books that people want to buy, but I don't know how to keep them coming in the door. I was thinking of starting a book club, maybe."

"Then do it. The sooner you start, the better off you're going to be," Les agreed.

"Thank God I'm closed tomorrow. I'm beat." Dex closed his eyes, and Les took his hand. "Starting a business… okay, keeping one going… is harder than I ever thought it would be. I mean, someone has to be in the store all the time, and I can't afford to hire anyone. Maybe eventually, if I can get the business built up, it'll get easier." He swallowed hard. "I was on the internet a little today and I read about how hard it is for small bookshops to survive." He squeezed Les's fingers. "I don't want to fail at this. It would be like letting my mother down, and I don't think I can do that."

"Then come up with what you think you need to do. Put up some book club sign-up sheets. Come up with reading areas. Bring in authors." Les put his foot down and leaned forward in his chair. "Do whatever you need to in order to make the store different from the big guys. It's going to take a lot. If this is something you really want, then don't go halfway." His expression was so serious. "Your mom made the store work, and so can you."

Dex nodded, but he couldn't help thinking about how his mother had made it work. If Les knew, he'd probably blow a gasket, but Dex was going to make it a success even if it killed him. But to do that, he needed more capital. Only an influx of cash would get things off the ground.

"Dinner is almost ready." Jane brought in a tray with some finger foods and beers.

"Sit down," Dex offered and tugged the chair a little closer. "You need to rest just as much as I do."

"Dinner has another fifteen minutes in the oven." She sat and put her feet up.

Dex opened and handed out the beers. "To Mom," he said softly, and all three of them clinked their bottles. "She really loved a good beer." He took a swig and swallowed. "And this definitely isn't one of them." He made a face, and the others did too. "Where did this come from?"

"One of the mourners brought it. She said that she and Sarah would each have one whenever Sarah visited her." Jane set her beer back on the tray, and the others did as well. "What I can't figure out is what they did to make it taste that awful."

"I have no idea." Les began reading the label. "They added sugar." He set the bottle aside.

Dex took the beers back into the kitchen, poured them down the sink, then found a couple bottles of Corona in the back of the refrigerator. He grabbed three of them, returned, and opened them.

"Let's try this again. To Mom… to Sarah," he said, and they drank. That was at least better. Beer should not taste like candy or cough syrup. Dex sat back down and placed his hand on Les's.

"You're shaking," Les whispered.

"I'm just stressed out." He had thought that the unknowns of Hollywood and show business were nerve-racking, but the store and the fickle winds of business were equally unnerving in a very different way. Add to that the little present that his mother had left for him and he kept wondering what the hell he was going to do.

Not that everything was all bad. He had a place to live and the rent from two apartments. That would mean that the building itself would bring in some cash each month. But now he was a landlord as well as a shopkeeper.

"Are you sure that's all it is?" Les asked. Dex nodded, sighing. Les was so strong, and Dex felt like he could lean on him. Sometimes it shocked him how easy it was to help someone else with their problems, and yet not have a clue how to handle your own.

"Yeah. I just have a lot of work to do." He smiled and pushed his worries away. Dex was here with Les and Jane, and he needed to leave business at the store and just enjoy some down time.

The oven dinged, and Jane got up. "Time to eat, boys. I didn't slave all evening to reheat this stuff for nothing," she quipped with a smile and left the room.

"Are you doing okay with all this? It's a lot of change," Les said. "You came back and found a store and a place to live, but are you doing this just because you think it's what your mother would have wanted?" He tugged his hand away as though he feared the answer. "The store was your mom's dream, and she kept it going for years. But it isn't something that you have to do just because she left it to you. You have your own dreams...."

Dex sighed. "That are going nowhere. And I doubt they ever will now." He wasn't sure what to do. "I can act, and I have a good look, but not the one that anyone is searching for. Every day I get older and my chances get smaller. I'm thirty-two, and in Hollywood I'm over the hill."

"There are plenty of older actors," Les protested.

"True. But they were young actors who got older. Tom Hanks is amazing, but he's been in the business for decades. And what? They're going to cast me over someone who's proven themself? It's just a hard life, and I'm getting tired of it." He closed his eyes. "I'm tired of being told that I'm not... whatever it is that they're looking for. So as you told me once, I think I need to find a different dream. The bookstore will allow me to be creative, and I get to meet different people. I think it could be good, but if it doesn't work out, at least I own the building. I could close the store and rent out the space to someone else." That idea seemed like betraying his mother, but it was a possibility. "What about you? Have you thought any more about what you'd like to do with your life now?"

Les shrugged. "I have some benefits I'm not using. Maybe I'll go back to school. Because I was injured on the job, there's some educational and retraining money that I could use."

"What sort of college are you interested in?" Jane asked as she returned with plates and silverware.

"I was thinking of law school. I have the undergraduate work all set, and it's within the same field, just from a different perspective. And my police background should work in my favor."

"It's a lot of work, but I bet you'd make a great lawyer," Dex said.

"I became a police officer because I wanted to help people, and I could do that as a lawyer. I'm smart and I understand the law. It would be different, but I'd like to think I'd have a leg up." He took the plate Jane offered, and she returned with a pasta dish and scooped out cheesy and saucy goodness that made the room smell like Italian heaven.

"Then do it. Would you go to Dickinson College here in town? They have a law program," Dex said. "I'm sure they would accept you."

Les nodded. "I'd have to take all the tests and then apply, but I could start in a year if I did well enough." He seemed excited, which pleased Dex. He liked it when Les got that way. His eyes sparkled and his lips drew upward. Les had this energy about him that radiated out into the room. "I need to look into it more closely."

"Then do it, by all means," Dex said. "Do you know anyone at the law school?"

"A few people. I worked with them when I was on the force. There were a few times when I needed to consult with attorneys, and the faculty at the school were always willing to help." It sounded to Dex as though Les had figured out a path forward. Now he just needed to do the same.

Chapter 7

LES AND Dex had decided to get together to do something on Sunday, but Dex hadn't let him in on exactly what. Instead, Dex had asked Les to leave it in his hands, and he had agreed.

Now that he was alone in his bed, he couldn't help thinking about Dex. He was sexy and hot, and the things that raced through Les's mind involved Dex writhing under him. The only problem was that every time he let his imagination run, it seemed to insert hollowed-out books into the scene. God, he was beginning to think his mind had slipped the tracks.

Les turned to his clock and groaned. It was three in the morning, and all he seemed to be able to think about was the paperback he had seen in the back of Dex's car, and what exactly it was being used for.

It had only been one book. Maybe he was making too much of it, but his cop's mind wouldn't leave it alone.

Maybe Dex had no idea what it was, and that got Les worrying that Dex was getting into something he wouldn't be able to handle. Needless to say, his mind was going in hamster wheel circles.

Les had been watching the bookstore before Sarah died, and he was pretty sure that she had been floating the business with a little illegal activity. He'd seen books being returned and exchanged. The times he had been in, he'd watched customers, but nothing had seemed out of place. The young people didn't seem to be acting the way he would expect if they were buying drugs. Yet something told him that there was something going on. He just hadn't been able to put his finger on it. Now that Dex had the business, Les really hoped he had been wrong. But after seeing that odd book, his suspicions were on alert.

The obvious answer was drugs of some type. But what exactly? Sarah hadn't come across as a coke dealer. Though when he had been on the force, he had seen stranger things than a retirement-age lady supplementing her income selling illicit substances.

Right now he just wished his head would settle. Dex was picking him up at ten, and at this rate he was going to fall asleep on the way to wherever they were going. Les turned on a light to see if reading would help. He wondered if he should simply ask Dex if he had found anything. How could he phrase that question? "Dex, do you think your mama was a drug dealer?" Or maybe, "Dex, did you find anything in the store that you shouldn't have, like a big bag of pills behind the counter or maybe a kilo of coke under the back of the toilet?" Yeah, that that was going to go over like a lead balloon… and Dex would likely never speak to him again. Les needed to realize that while he could have his suspicions, that was all he had.

Let it go. If something was going on, the police would figure it out. And if there was nothing to find, his questions weren't going to cost him someone he was really beginning to care about.

Les was about to give up and turn out the light when his phone vibrated, and he picked it up, expecting it to be a message from Facebook for something.

What are you doing up?

Les smiled as he answered Red's message. I guess I'm just that predictable. Red was a seasoned officer, and he, along with Harry, had taken Les under his wing when he'd been a rookie. Les had been lucky to have two great officers see something in him, and they had remained friends when Les was injured. You must be working the night shift.

Yeah, and when I saw the light on in your place, I figured it was a safe bet that you were up, Red texted. So I thought I'd take a chance.

When is your break? Les asked. When Red told him he could take one anytime, he replied, I'll start some coffee. Then he pushed back the covers, got out of bed, and left the bedroom.

The rest of the apartment was warm, so he opened the windows to allow the night air inside. He started the coffee and went down the back to let Red inside. They didn't talk as they climbed the stairs once again because he didn't want to disturb his neighbors.

"What has you up so late?" Red asked once Les closed the door.

"I can't turn my head off sometimes," he explained. "See, I met someone. His mother owned the bookstore across the street."

"Sarah's son." Red nodded and sat down. He was a big man with scars across his cheeks. Not that Les really saw them any longer. They'd drawn his attention when he and Red had first met, but now it was Red's steady nature and good heart that really mattered. If Red hadn't already been spoken for, Les might have expressed interest in him at one time. "I hear he's going to keep the store open."

"It looks like it." Les hoped he did and that his suspicions were wrong. "The thing is… before Sarah died, I…." God, he hated suspecting a dead woman. "That store couldn't have done enough business to sustain itself. After I got hurt, I used to sit in that window. With nothing to do, I used to count the number of customers who went inside." It sounded stupid, but it was something he did when he was bored. As a kid he used to count the ceiling tiles in his school classrooms, and when his mom was punishing him, the bricks in the wall in front of him. It gave his mind something to do.

"What do you suspect?" Red asked.

"Well… she used to have maybe two or three customers a day for weeks on end. There was no way the sale of a few books a day was going to keep the store running. She needed more than that, and I wondered if she was doing something to supplement her income. But it was just a feeling I had." Les got up and poured Red a mug of coffee, moving carefully. He handed it to Red and sat back down. If he had some, he'd never get to sleep the rest of the night. "I never had any proof of wrongdoing, and I was coming to believe that it had all just been my imagination."

"Then she passed away, and you met her son?" Red sipped his coffee. "And from what I hear, you like the guy." He smirked. "Tyler told Terry about your evening while they were talking at the gym. Apparently, according to Tyler, the guy is hot."

"Yeah, he is." Les felt color rising to his cheeks. "But…." He yawned, and Red drank some more of the coffee.

"Sarah is gone, and whatever she may have been doing died with her. I know you have the singlemindedness of a bloodhound most of the time, but if you want my advice, let this go. I really doubt Sarah was into anything illegal, and if she was, it's in the past now. Criminals can be anyone, but really… does Dex seem the type to you?

If his mother was supplementing her income, it doesn't mean that Dex is as well."

"No. But…."

"Have you seen anything incriminating?"

Les shook his head. Yeah, the hollowed-out book was suspicious, but it wasn't incriminating. It could simply be a book safe. Maybe the bookstore carried such things. "Not really. I spent some time in the store before she passed away, and the people I'd suspect of being customers for that kind of thing did nothing suspicious. In fact, I saw nothing out of the ordinary. People would talk to Sarah, they bought books, and then they left. She was a really nice lady."

"Then there you go." Red finished his coffee and set the mug on the table. "Sometimes it's best if you just move on. You like Dex, right?"

Les nodded. "Yeah. We're supposed to get together in the morning, and we've been seeing each other quite a bit."

"Then don't rock the boat for a hunch that could be wrong. Remember, cops follow the trail of evidence. Yeah, we have a sixth sense sometimes, but we can't follow it blindly or we end up trampling on someone's rights. In this case, you could hurt someone you care for." Red checked the time on his phone and stood. "I'm well aware of the problems that we have with drugs in this town. I see it every day. So while I'm not saying this lightly…." He smiled warmly as Les. "Let yourself be happy. If Dex brings you happiness, then go with it. Don't let some suspicion about his mother color your impression of him. If something was going on at the store, we would have heard about it from a suspect. I've talked to a lot of people involved with drugs in this town, but there has never been a whisper about the bookstore. Other businesses, definitely, and we've shut them down hard. But never even a whisper about Sarah."

Les hadn't known how Red would react, but he didn't expect this. Maybe he needed to try to go at it from another angle. "Is there anything happening with the drug case I was working on?" That was still a sore subject with him, since it had resulted in him being laid up. But if Les could solve it, maybe he could get the force to take another look at him. He was still a police officer, after all. Maybe he could be part of the team, even if it was in a different capacity.

Red growled. "We're getting nowhere fast, and that has the chief angry. They always seem to be one step ahead of us. You're the only one who got anywhere close." The implications of what the felons involved in the drug ring were capable of hung silently in the air, just as Les's foot chose that moment to throb as a reminder.

This conversation was only making him feel worse. Better to think of something good, even though it was hard for his mind to give up on something once he got his teeth into it. "I do really like Dex. He's fun."

"Then enjoy it and don't worry about what might already be in the past. I need to get back on duty, and you should go to bed. Let yourself relax and indulge in some of the good things in life. You deserve them. And if he makes you happy, worrying about what his mother might have done isn't going to get you anywhere." He sighed and shrugged. "What are you going to do if it's true? Tell him and ruin his memories of his mom? Somehow bring charges against him for things done before he even got back to town? The only thing you'll do is ruin the store for him—the one he's already put a lot of effort into. No one is going to come out well in this, especially not you." He headed toward the door. "Thanks for the coffee."

"Thanks for the advice," Les said with a smile. "Maybe we can get together again soon."

"That would be great."

Red left, and Les locked the door before turning out the light and going back to bed. Red was right. He was worrying about something that was in the past. With his mind settled, Les climbed under the covers in the cool room and finally went to sleep.

"ARE YOU going to tell me where we're going?" Les got into Dex's car, sliding his cane next to his legs.

"Nope," Dex told him with a smile. "But I suspect you'll figure it out soon enough." He pulled away from the curb and out on Hanover Street, the main road going south.

"Gettysburg?" Les guessed.

"That was pretty easy," Dex said as he continued through town.

"There isn't all that much south of here, unless we were going to Mt. Holly or York Springs."

Dex chuckled. "I thought we could have a nice lunch when we get there and maybe stop at one of the farm markets on the way home. The cherries should be in by now. There could also be a few other things available, even though it's a little early in the season."

"Cherries?" Les asked, rubbing his hands. "I love them."

"Then we'll see." Dex passed through the lights by Home Depot, and then they were outside of town. The houses grew fewer and the land opened up to farms and mountains in the distance. "I figured we could just have some fun today. We don't have to do all the Civil War stuff if you don't want to."

Les settled contentedly in the seat. "The first time I went to Gettysburg, I was in middle school. We had a tour of the battlefield, and they took us to the top of the hill. I remember that because we were finally able to get out of the bus and run around." Being cooped up in that bus for hours while the teacher rambled on about this battle and that general had been torture. Once they were free of the bus, they had swarmed the hill like cooped-up locusts, running in every direction. It had been so much fun.

"I went when I was in sixth grade. This guy at the cemetery was dressed up as Abraham Lincoln, and he recited the Gettysburg Address and even answered questions. It was cool. The kids tried to trip him up, but he answered as Abraham Lincoln, always in character. It was such a great day. And we got to see the cyclorama painting, which was pretty cool. I don't remember much else about that trip. It was a long time ago."

"Have you been back since?" Les asked, noticing Dex's eyes momentarily darken. Then the look was gone. He wondered if something happened on that particular trip.

"No. I've been through town, but that's all. How about you?"

"The same. When you live here, it isn't like you do all the touristy things," Les agreed. "I've been to a few places to eat, though. Did you have someplace in mind? If not, I can offer a recommendation." It was good to think about food instead of the battlefield. If they went on a tour, he'd undoubtedly hear about all the war injuries and how they were treated. Those images bothered him now, where they hadn't before the accident. He hated to admit it, but talking about the kind of stuff he'd invariably hear on a tour would likely remind him of how close he'd come to losing his foot altogether. Les didn't want to rain on Dex's parade.

"We could go to the Dobbin House, if you like. There are a few other places, but I like it there. It's on a lower level, so it's always cool, and their food is pretty good. The other places in town are mostly burgers and things like that."

"That was the one I intended to suggest. I've never been and always wanted to try it." Les forced a smile. Dex was so excited, and it wasn't like they were going to be talking battlefields and injuries at lunch. He just hated the cloud that seemed to have settled over him. He decided that he was going to have a good time if it killed him. Les looked the restaurant up and checked their website. The place didn't offer reservations, so he and Dex might have to wait, but that was fine with him.

They passed through Mt. Holly and York Springs and then Biglerville, with its apple-shaped street lights. Continuing on, they approached the outskirts of Gettysburg, where there were lines of monuments through the fields. "Do you think we can go to the top of Little Round Top?" It offered a great view of the whole valley. He remembered that from when he was a kid. Les just hoped he would be able to get around.

"Of course," Dex said. "I wanted this to be a fun day. There isn't a schedule—we can do whatever you like. Though we don't have to go to the Hall of Presidents or on one of those ghost tours unless you really want to."

"I think we can skip that," Les agreed as they passed Gettysburg College and the Lincoln train station and made the roundabout at the center of town. The place really was like a throwback in time. There were bars and gift shops, as well as antique stores and militaria stores. It was an eclectic mix that got even more touristy the closer they got to the military cemetery. There, the streets were lined with T-shirt stores, fudge and candy shops, and even costume shops. "Wow, I hadn't realized it had gotten quite this bad. I mean, ice cream I can see, but everything else…. You'd think this was Ocean City or something." He made a face as Dex continued driving.

Eventually they pulled into the parking lot of the restaurant. The lot was really full, but as they came around, a car was backing out, so Dex waited, and they slipped into the parking space. "This was a nice idea." He leaned over the console, and Dex kissed him quickly before the intense sun heated the car to a furnace.

"I've never eaten here, though I think I've heard about the Dobbin House almost my entire life. Mom and Dad used to come here before Dad died, and they always talked about the onion soup and how special the place was. I guess I wanted to see what this was like," Dex admitted.

Les grinned. "An adventure."

Dex's laugh turned to a snort. "We aren't heading out in the wilderness to hunt us some wild boar." They opened the heavy, old door and walked inside. Les followed Dex toward the stairs, looking down.

"So, we're just going down a narrow set of twisted stone stairs, hoping the guy with the cane doesn't fall and take out three little old ladies and a busboy." Les wagged his eyebrows and slowly made his way downward, thankful when he reached the bottom. "Do I get extra points for taking out a tourist?" He had to cover how jittery he'd felt on those stairs.

Dex rolled his eyes. "Only if you knock them out of their shoes."

In the dining room, each table had a candle, and two of the walls were cut out of stone and lit from below. It was interesting but rather dark. Les sat at the table the hostess directed them to and checked out one of the paper menus. The tables were rustic and the ceiling low and beamed. It was very much a room out of the eighteenth century.

"Is it okay?" Dex asked once they had sat down.

"Sure." Les smiled as Dex caught his gaze. The room buzzed with conversation, but it was low, the dimness encouraging softer discussion. "It's just different from what I expected." He stretched out his leg and sighed softly, turning to the side so he could prop his leg up on the bench.

"How so?" Dex asked. "I couldn't help noticing something. You've been different during the last part of the drive, and you're tenser than you were at home." He leaned closer. "Something is bothering you. Is it the restaurant? The stairs? If you didn't want to come, all you had to do was say so and we could have done something else."

He sounded a little perturbed, and the look he gave Les reminded him of the one his old football coach had shot him when he'd caught Les skipping practice before the biggest game of the year. His jaw set, and Les realized he just needed to be up-front.

"I remember the last time I was here. We were on a bus tour, and they spent a lot of time talking about injuries and how they treated them and…"

Dex gasped and put his hand to his mouth. "Okay. Here's the deal. We are going to have a nice day, and there will be no talk about Civil War medicine or anything that even borders on the icky. With all the happy tourist stuff outside, it's easy to forget the real reason this place is famous." He sighed. "I'm so stupid sometimes. I wanted this to be a fun outing… so I brought you to a battlefield." He shook his head and they both chuckled.

Les felt himself relax, more determined than ever to have to a good time. Maybe what he needed to do was change the subject. "I've been meaning to ask you if you've found any surprises in the store."

Dex stiffened. "Like what?"

Les hadn't meant to blurt that out quite so bluntly, so he backpedaled a little. "Just something you didn't realize was there. You've been gone a while, and your mom had an eccentric side. I just thought you might have come across something unexpected. And I've heard that sometimes, in going through a parent's things, it's not surprising to find things you thought were gone a long time ago."

"Oh yeah. I rummaged through some of the old boxes in the back and found some of the things I put in the windows. There's a whole set of Winnie the Pooh stuffies that I remembered playing with a few times as a kid. They were all there. Mom kept a lot of stuff and packed it into one of the closets. There were boxes neatly stacked from floor to ceiling. I haven't had a chance to go through them all yet." He seemed to have relaxed now and patted Les's hand on the table. "I'm glad I decided to stay."

"Me too," Les agreed.

"When I was a kid, I couldn't wait to get out of this town. I graduated and left for the West Coast, as soon as I could. I was going to be discovered, become famous, and then come back and show everyone in town just how far I had gone." He sat up straighter, and the way his eyes sparkled was adorable. "None of it worked out that way, but I'm back anyway."

"There's something soothing about being back in your hometown," Les offered. "I thought of moving away, figuring there had to be more out there for me to see. It turned out that what I wanted was right back here." He shrugged. "Though I do dream of traveling someday. I think I'd like to see Paris and Rome, places like that. Have a chance to experience some of the world. But when I'm done, I want to be able to come home again. Did you get to go anywhere other than LA?"

Dex shook his head. "I thought that my trip to California would be the beginning and that I could see the world from there. The closest I got was Little Tokyo."

Just then, their server came over. "May I take your order?" he asked.

Les pulled his attention to the menu. He ordered a Coke and a roast beef sandwich with potato salad and some of the restaurant's famous onion soup. Dex got chicken and coleslaw. Then the server bustled to the next table.

"But LA must have been interesting," Les asked, curious what Dex's life had been like.

"There were plenty of things to do, and it could be a lot of fun. But I spent most of my time trying to line up auditions or working to make ends meet. I thought that the streets would be paved with gold, but I was killing myself just to make a basic living and to somehow keep my head above water. The last call I got sent on was for porn, and before that, I was up for the part of producer's cute boyfriend to take to parties… and of course sleep with. No. My career there was going nowhere. I wanted to act because I love it. But the business and all its ugliness just seemed to get in the way." He squeezed Les's fingers. "It's a lot easier here. People are friendly and aren't so driven all the time." He leaned over the table. "And I never met a guy like you out there, that's for sure."

Les felt his cheeks heat a little. "Come on."

"Oh, there were hot-looking guys, but they all knew they were hot-looking. People spent most of the time looking past you. You'd go out with someone, and a lot of the time they were looking to see if there was someone hotter to be with, someone more… I don't know. It was just too much."

Les didn't understand that at all. If he was with someone, that was it. "How can someone do that?" he asked. "Okay… sometimes there are guys who are better-looking than any of us. But…." He shrugged. "That seems so shallow and ridiculous."

"Some of it was. But I was trying to work in Hollywood, the shallow, self-centered capital of the world. It was how it was." He sighed and sat back in his chair as the server brought their drinks and Les's soup. "But I'm more content here. I'm sad that it took Mom's passing to help me see it."

"Sometimes opportunities come at the weirdest times." He squeezed Dex's hand.

"I miss her. There are so many things I'd like to ask her, about the store, about her life…. There's so much I missed out on because I was trying to make it big… and that didn't happen." He swallowed, and Les took a spoonful of his soup. "Sometimes I wonder if all that time was wasted."

Les shook his head. "Everything that happened to you—and that you did—has made you the person you are today. Sometimes we have to fail at something before we can really understand what success is." He rolled his eyes and smiled. "Listen to me. I sound like the great oracle of Carlisle, and I don't know crap about anything. I sit in my apartment feeling sorry for myself because I don't do what I used to. Hell, I spent months like that."

"Why did you stop?" Dex asked.

"Because I found something to go out for," Les admitted around the lump in his throat. "Who would have thought that someone I met when he was going through a huge loss would help bring me back to life? It's ironically strange."

"I guess you never know." Dex sat back as the server brought the rest of their order. The dining area filled quickly, and soon the room became much louder. "I always expected this place to be bigger."

"There's the gift shop and a banquet space on the main floor, as well as other rooms that are set up as a museum of sorts." Les pointed to the information on the menu. "Apparently this was also a stop on the underground railroad." He couldn't help shaking his head.

"What?"

Les shrugged. "I was just thinking of some of the things I saw when I was a cop. The way people can treat each other can turn your stomach sometimes. I've seen children hurt and wives hit by husbands. I've seen people shoot one another over a pair of tennis shoes. But…." He sighed. "Individual acts of violence are nothing when compared to what people have done to each other when the cruelty is institutionalized."

Dex leaned over the table. "And you think it isn't now?" He took a bite of his sandwich.

"Of course it is now," Les said. "My last partner was a real problem. He and I were complete opposites. I was young and idealistic, while he was about fifty, with a lot of experience. The problem was that it was the wrong kind of experience… at least for me." Les finished his soup and set the bowl aside. "The pairing was a huge mistake. I can see that now. I should have talked to my supervisor about it or outright refused to be paired with him. I'd have been better off alone." He took a small bite of his sandwich.

"Did he have a problem with you being gay?"

"He had a problem with anyone and everyone who was different from him. He didn't say anything about gay people, at least to me, but he listened to all that conservative talk radio all the time, and he hated Muslims. Hell, he hated anyone of color. I saw him acting extra harsh with black suspects. I gathered a list of grievances and thought about taking it to the captain, but you don't turn on a brother. That's the code. I could have turned him in, but then most of the department would have turned their backs on me. Maybe not all of the guys, but a lot. I was trying to figure out what to do when I was injured." Les hadn't realized he had been holding on to his sandwich until he put it back on the plate.

"Is he still on the force?" Dex asked.

"As far as I know, though Red and some of the other guys have told me that he's under pressure to change his ways. He's giving cops a bad name, and the other guys don't want to deal with that sort of crap." Les was pleased that changes were happening. He only wished they had happened earlier.

Dex took another bite and seemed to be thinking. "I have to ask, though I've probably read too many books…. Isn't your partner supposed to have your back?"

"Of course. That's the idea. We often work in pairs so someone else is there to see what we can't." An arctic chill went up his back. Shit. Details about the night he'd been hurt solidified in his mind.

Les paused and his mouth opened to deny the idea that took root in his mind, but he realized he couldn't. It was indeed possible that Williams hadn't had his back that night—that Les could have been injured because he'd turned away. Even for a guy like Williams, that was a lot to think about. "I don't really want to admit he'd do something like that." Unfortunately, the details of that day were still fuzzy, though what Dex said made him think, even though he couldn't put his finger on exactly why.

He also couldn't let it go. "Jesus…," he breathed, as suddenly a lot more of the picture fell into place. "My partner didn't shoot me, but the fucker didn't do anything to stop it either." The curses that played through his mind would put the saltiest sailor to shame. "If that fucker planned this…. How could he?" Les needed to keep his mind clear and think like an investigator.

"What if he didn't plan it? What if he just turned away and didn't help you? That's possible, isn't it?" Dex shook his head. "Maybe I shouldn't have said anything. It isn't like I have any evidence. It was just a feeling. I hate the thought of anyone hurting you." His eyes darkened for a few seconds.

Les released a breath he'd been holding, going over the incident in his mind once again like he had a million times. Only this time he concentrated on Williams and what he had been doing.

Maybe Les had been stupid not to consider Williams's action in all this… or his lack of action. It was difficult to remember those details, especially after he'd been shot. The pain and trauma colored his memories, and he wished they were clearer. Not that he really wanted to think that his partner, a fellow police officer, would act that way, but the more he thought about it, the more the possibility took root. He wished he could get answers, but it wasn't like Williams was going to give him any. What was he going to do, admit it? "Oh yeah, I remember when you were shot. I nearly shit myself and couldn't do a thing to protect you. Sorry." Or worse, admit that he'd just stood there and let it happen? One less fag on the force—that would have been his attitude.

Les needed some time to figure out how to proceed. After all, he was here with Dex, and it wasn't like he could do anything in the moment anyway. He needed to come up with a plan to prove what happened either way.

Les calmed himself, letting the trained police officer step forward in his mind, as opposed to the emotional victim. He'd played that role long enough. "Well, I've had plenty of hurt and disappointments in my life. I think it's unavoidable. We live, we get hurt, feel pain, but sometimes, if we're lucky, we find someone who will love us. You had that. Your mom and Jane loved you."

"And your parents?"

"Oh, they love me, but they have their own lives. Mom and Dad figured that once I was an adult, their jobs were done and it was their chance to rediscover their own lives. I really can't blame them for that. They did the best they could for me, and the whole gay thing was a disappointment for them. Mom always wanted more grandchildren, and even today, when we talk, she'll ask if I've met someone who will help give her another little one."

"So your mom wants a grandbaby and she doesn't really care how she gets it?" Dex teased. "My mom dreamed of one too. I think when I came out to her, that was her only disappointment. Then her life changed and I think she came to understand things a little more clearly. But I could tell whenever I came to visit and saw her in the store with the little kids… that look on her face… it was pure yearning. She wanted someone to spoil and be a grandma to." Dex finished his sandwich and ate his salad. "I'd maybe like to have a child, now that I think about it. But here… it's still problematic."

"I thought of adopting a kid who needs a home." Les wasn't afraid to admit that. "As a police officer, I saw so many kids who desperately needed someone to care for them. A couple of the guys on the force have kids with their partners. Carter has Alex, and another officer looks after his sister's kids because she isn't able to. They're some of the best officers I know, and I wish I had been partnered with either of them. If I had, maybe things would have different." He finished his meal and caught the server's attention for the bill. "You know, maybe we should talk about something a little less heavy. We're having a day out. We could try having fun."

Dex smiled. "Amen to that. Let's drive around and look at the monuments for a while, then head on up to Little Round Top and have a look around. And on the way out, if you don't mind, I'd like to stop at the Christmas store in town. Jane has an amazing collection of nutcrackers that she puts out each year, and I'd like to find one for her. Maybe we could do some holiday shopping a little early."

"That's fine with me. It's a nice day." And he really just wanted a few hours of relaxation where he could forget about his foot and everything else.

The server brought their check, and Dex grabbed it before Les had a chance. Once it was paid, they left by the back stairs, which were just as steep, and went out through the museum portion of the building. "The hiding place for the underground railroad is up there."

Les slowly climbed the few stairs and peered into a space under part of the floor behind a small shelf that swung out. It was a little over two feet high, with a bedrock floor. The cramped space only made him think of how scary and uncomfortable it would be in there. Les hated the idea and stepped back down the stairs. It went to show what people would do for the chance at a better life.

Dex took a look too, saying he was suddenly claustrophobic, and then they continued outside and back to the car, which had become an oven. Les waited outside while Dex started the engine to cool things down, and then they went back through town. They turned down one of the roads lined with monuments to the regiments that fought during the three-day battle.

"When I was a kid, I was fascinated by this place. I used to ask Mom and Dad to take me to the reenactments, but they never did. They were always crowded and happened at the hottest time of the year. My folks just didn't want to deal with that. Now, it's simply sad. So many people died here, and it makes me wonder just how people can be so cruel to one another." He tried not to think about all the men who had lost their lives over an institution that should never have been allowed in the first place. It made him angry. Then Les realized he needed to get himself under control, because Dex had brought them here to have a little fun, and not….

"You're shaking."

"I thought I could enjoy this, but I don't think I can," Les said. "Maybe we can do something else?"

Dex pulled off the road. "Are you okay?" His voice was filled with concern.

"I will be." Les didn't understand where this pall was coming from, but it seemed almost palpable. This place shouldn't be affecting him like that. What had happened here was a long time ago, yet it seemed very real to him. "Maybe that's it."

"What's it?" Dex restarted the car and continued out to the back road.

"Well, I've seen tons of bad stuff in my work, and getting shot was, and still is, a nightmare for me. Maybe what I need to do is try to make that better, to move beyond all that. I don't know how yet, but perhaps a good way to start is to try to correct some of the things that are wrong. I mean, if I want the world to be a better place for everyone—the main reason I became a police officer in the first place—maybe I need to do something about it." He settled back in the seat, grateful that he had finally made a decision, and some of the agitation that always seemed to be present finally settled.

"How do you want to do that?" Dex asked. "You could advocate."

"No. I think I want to work with the police as well as the community. Help the officers see all people as people. Maybe help the community see the police as partners. But I think it's the police that have to change, if for no other reason than because of the perceptions… which I don't think are wrong, but they don't apply to everyone. There are super good cops… just like there are asshole cops. And Lord knows I got partnered with one of those." He smiled. "I'm just not sure how I'll go about it yet, but at least I know what I want to try to do."

"Then go for it," Dex said. "It sounds like what you want to do is exactly what's needed. Now figure out how to make it into something you'd love." He squeezed Les's knee as they slid into a parking space at the main square in town. "The store is down the street a little way. Is it too far for you to walk?"

"No." Les got out of the car and filled the parking meter. Then he and Dex walked down toward the shop.

Les had been expecting a typical tourist store, but this was anything but. All the items were traditional imported German items, and they were stunning. Handmade nutcrackers, glass ornaments that shimmered and sparkled on the trees, Christmas pyramids, nativities, and so much more, all glittering to holiday music. It was Christmas in June.

"Okay. This is…." He picked up a smoker of a hunter in a blind with his hunting dog. "My mom had some things like this when I was a kid."

"Some of these figures have been made for hundreds of years. They started in the south of Germany with its woodcarving tradition. A lot of the original designs are Black Forest, like the clocks. But some are from other regions with various traditions." The woman behind the counter smiled as she explained. "These just scream Christmas to me."

"To me too," Dex said as he picked up a few nutcrackers. Les glanced at the prices, and his eyes widened. Most of them were close to two hundred dollars.

"This is for Jane," Dex said softly. He set one that had a crown and ermine cape on the counter. "She really deserves a queen." The clerk got the box, and Dex paid for it while Les continued looking around.

Everything in this store was way more than he could afford for a holiday that was six months off. Les was still getting his life together and waiting for his permanent disability to be approved. Still, looking around the store was fun, and he met Dex at the door once his package had been wrapped and he was ready to go. "You're opening the bookstore tomorrow?"

"Yeah. We'll see how business is. I was thinking of closing on Mondays as well as Sunday to give myself two days off. But I'll have to see how the day goes." He put the nutcracker in the trunk. "Do you want to see what else there is? Or we can head out and stop at some of the fruit stands between here and home."

"I don't know what there is."

"I think the important issue is what your foot is up to." Dex stood right in front of him. "I've seen the way you're moving. If your foot hurts, we can just head on back toward Carlisle."

"I'm fine," Les said, even as his foot chose that time to offer a painful throb. He was so tired of not being able to do the things he wanted. "Let's go over there. I think I saw some interesting stores as we went around the circle." He started across the street and continued down to a couple of gift shops and a military antiques store. In the back, they had some reproduction uniforms. He held a few up to Dex, knowing he'd look incredible in something like that.

"You got a thing for uniforms?" Dex whispered. Les may have nodded. "I bet you have one or two that you look really good in."

"I see. You like cops, do you?"

Dex smirked and leaned close. "Firemen, marines, sailors… there's something about seafood, but cops, yeah, I think they're sexy." His gaze heated in seconds, and it took all of Les's restraint not to tug Dex into a kiss right there in the store.

"So you'd like it if I were to show you what I look like in one of my uniforms?"

Dex nodded. "Though I think you'd look a lot better out of one of those uniforms. Maybe in one of those shirts with the long tails and a badge, your powerful legs jutting out to the floor. Now that would be a sight worthy of walking across a desert for."

Les lowered his voice. "I see. You like the long 'arm' of the law." He smirked. "They always say Les is more." Dex grinned and rolled his eyes, the perfect reaction to Les's cheesiness. "Well, then. We'll have to see what we can do to make that happen. But we have things to do first. Like finish up in this store before we both embarrass ourselves." Les glanced to the older man behind the counter giving them the evil eye. Then he smirked and tried unsuccessfully to hold in the naughty-kid laugh as he made his way toward the door and outside.

"Kids today," the man behind the counter muttered as Les stepped outside and back into the early summer heat. It hit him hard, and he began making his way back toward the car. Les's energy flagged as the discomfort in his foot grew. He kept looking ahead toward where they had parked the car.

"Les...."

"I'm okay," he said firmly and continued forward, using his cane to take more of his weight. Dex unlocked the car, and Les slid into the seat, sighing as soon as the weight was off his foot. He'd overdone it, and he knew he was going to pay for it later. And he'd probably have to take some meds.

Cool air flowed almost as soon as Dex started the engine and pulled out of the parking spot. Les kept his eyes closed as the pressure in his foot slowly dissipated and his breathing returned to normal. "If you just want to go home, I can do that," Dex offered.

"No. Let's stop at the farm market." He didn't want to ruin the day. There were times when Les really wanted to be normal again— the man he was before the accident.

Except maybe it hadn't been an accident. That thought crept back into his head, and it wouldn't go away. As he rode, sitting quietly in the passenger seat, he thought back to that night again and again, willing his mind to pull out additional details from the fog of pain, but nothing came.

The tires rumbled as they passed over the railroad tracks on the edge of town, pulling Les out of his head, at least for a few moments. He blinked and glanced at Dex, who was concentrating on the road with such intensity that Les thought he might have been memorizing the horizon. "Let's get you back so you can put your foot up."

Les placed his hand on Dex's leg, appreciating his concern and care. "I'm okay. I overdid it a little. Maybe when we're at the market, they'll have something cold to drink or even a farm café or something." He breathed deeply and slowly, willing the pain to go away and hoping he wasn't sweating all over the seat of the car.

There were so many things going on right now—his foot, his mind reopening the accident in a way he never thought about... because of Dex's question. And too, there was the stuff going on at the store that his head refused to let go of. He wished he could make it quiet, but when something got under his skin, it didn't go away. Les watched out the windows as the townscape shifted back to fields of monuments and then farms and trees.

"What's bothering you?" Dex asked. "Your leg is bouncing and you're muttering under your breath."

"Nothing." He pushed his circling thoughts away to get his head back to the here and now.

"I'm sorry for what I said at the restaurant. I had no right to ask if your partner could have been involved in your accident. I think I've spent too much time with movie and television scripts. Those sorts of things would be what happened in fiction. If I upset you, I didn't mean to. I…."

Les shook his head. "It was okay. I didn't think that. In fact, just the opposite. The idea never occurred to me, and it should have. I keep going over what happened again and again, and I come up with nothing. I can't remember where Williams was or what he was doing. I know he was there, and that's about all. The details are fuzzy, especially once I was hurt." He stopped his hand from shaking.

"Who else was there?"

"Just the suspects. But they were the guys who shot me. I doubt they'd be of any help." Les figured he was going to have to let this go. Any time an officer was shot, there was an investigation.

"Can I ask something? Why not get one of your friends to talk to those guys? They're in custody, right? I know it sounds very Hollywood, but they might be willing to talk—especially if they know it will go bad for another cop." Damn, Dex could be devious.

"I can ask Red. He's a good guy and someone I trust. But I have a feeling he'll tell me that this is a ridiculous idea." He hoped so. If Williams was actually involved or negligent, it would open a whole can of shit that could end up flying everywhere. That was an image he tried not to let take hold in his head.

"There's the farm market."

Les smiled as Dex pulled off and into the parking lot. He got out, and they slowly looked things over. As they suspected, it was somewhat early in the season, but they had a lot of lettuce and some beans, as well as cherries. Dex seemed to be getting quite a few. "Jane loves sweet cherries, and I want to get something to cheer her up."

"You're really worried about her," Les observed.

"Losing Mom is hard, and I'm going to miss her a great deal. But for Jane, Mom was her entire world… and now she's gone. Jane had a hard life before she met Mom, and they made each other so very happy. Can you imagine waking up and suddenly realizing you're all alone?"

"You can still be lonely in a room full of people," Les observed as he selected some beans and a quart of cherries. He set them on one of the checkout counters before he finished looking around. One of the things about the cane was that he didn't have his hands free the way others did.

"Yes, you can. But Jane is lonely and alone, and I think that only makes things worse." He added his own choice of items to Les's, and they finished looking things over. Fortunately, there was a cooler of cold drinks, and Les got one for himself and for Dex and added them to their order before the cashier rang them up. Dex carried their purchases to the car and set them in the back seat for the rest of the ride home.

"Tell me something about you that I don't know," Les asked once they were on the road again. "Something you don't usually share with others."

"Okay. I lived in California and I didn't like the water. I'd go to the ocean and never go in. All I could imagine were the jellyfish, sharks, and other nasty things that could be lurking beneath the waves. I don't want people to think I'm crazy, so I never mention it. You?"

"I love the water," Les teased. "But I guess I could say that I'm a huge fan of Downton Abbey. I love the period dramas, and I can't get enough of the interactions between the characters."

"I see," Dex said. "I watched a couple of seasons and gave it up. I don't think it was for me. Though I do have some questions. One of the main characters, the earl… why is his wife a countess? He isn't a count."

"No. The equivalent title on the continent is a count," Les supplied.

"Okay. But how come his wife isn't an earl-ess?" Dex grinned. "Oh, I like earlerina. The Earlerina of Snuffington."

"How about earlette?" Les postulated with a grin. God, he loved it when Dex smiled. All the worry and pain slipped away and Dex seemed to come alive. He was seeing more of that, and it drew him closer.

"Better yet, earline. Now that sounds regal." Dex added his own mischievous grin, and Les flashed one right back. That was sexy.

Suddenly Les wished they were a lot closer to his place. Dex turned up the air-conditioning to cool the car a little more.

"It sounds like a kind of cat." Les was definitely getting a kick out of this.

"Yeah. Well, you've seen the show. Lady Mary would definitely qualify as an earline. That was one catty character." Dex adjusted the vent, and Les wondered how this talk about Downton Abbey could make him hot. Maybe he had a kink for titles or something.

"You seem to know a lot about the show for someone who has only seen the first couple of seasons," Les pressed.

"It was all the rage, and there was talk of a number of period pieces like that in Hollywood. I figured I'd work on an accent and see if I could get a part. You need to be a bit of a chameleon if you want to get ahead out there. God, if you look at some of the things that people come up with. Thankfully most of them never make it out of the idea stage, but sometimes you never know what the next super-hit is going to be. And if you're an actor who's barely making ends meet, you do whatever you need to."

"That must have been terrible," Les said, patting Dex's leg. "I know who I am, but to try to change parts of yourself to fit what you thought someone else wanted must have torn at you."

Dex shrugged. "I'm an actor. It's what we do and what I love. When we take on a role, part of us becomes that character, at least for a time. I could be an earl or a duke… or even a rent boy for a while. I've been a tortured Southern man trying to fight his homosexuality, as well as a party boy out for a good time. I played a retiree and a middle-aged vacuum-cleaner salesman. A few times I played dead bodies. That was about as much fun as you can imagine. But all of them had their challenges, and, well, other than the bodies, I got to figure out what made the character tick. Even the bad guys are the heroes of their own story, and their story was mine to discover, even if it wasn't actually part of the scene. Think about it." He began talking faster as his thoughts tumbled out. "There are times when I was playing a character that had been presented dozens of times before. But for that day, that character was my responsibility, my charge, and I got to be the one to make my Hamlet, or my Romeo, unique and imbue those roles with a part of me." Dex seemed more excited and he grinned broadly as he braked behind a semi just in front of them. "Looks like we're not going anywhere fast."

That was true. They slowed and stayed in a line of cars behind the truck, which could only go so fast on the curvy road that went up and over hills. Fortunately, they weren't in a hurry. It took almost an hour before they approached the outskirts of Carlisle and the road widened enough that they were able to pass the truck.

"Do you mind if we stop at the store?" Dex asked.

"Of course not." Les settled back in his seat, and they drove through town and to the rear entrance of the building. They entered through the back door, and Les found himself in the small private room. There were shelves and a few boxes, along with a couple of doors, one he assumed led to the basement.

"I'll be right back." Dex hurried out front.

Les couldn't help doing a little snooping. Everything was neat and orderly. He leaned against a table, sighing softly. He knew he should just wait for Dex and let that be the end of it. But he had to figure out what was going on. He wished he'd never glimpsed that damned hollowed-out book. He wandered through the space, not seeing anything out of the ordinary. Of the few boxes that he casually peered into, one held book stands and the other paperbacks. Les pulled one out and thumbed through the romance, then slid the book back in before picking out another. This one had a woman in a huge gown that flowed to the floor. He peered inside and found a hollowed-out space.

Once again, he couldn't help wondering what these books could be used for. They were older and the edges discolored, as though they had seen a lot of use.

Without thinking, he brought the book to his nose. The faint traces of marijuana tickled his senses. He knew that heavy, pungent scent anywhere, and while what he smelled was faint, it was there. One of the properties of pot was that it was oily, and that oil clung to anything it came in contact with, leaving traces of scent that clung to surfaces.

He had no way of knowing how recently this book had been used, but it seemed as if his hunch was right. Now Les just had to figure out what he was going to do with the information. If it was just pot, was it that big a deal? He didn't think the drug ring he'd been investigating would bother with something as inconsequential as pot. And his discovery today wouldn't do anything to help him get back on the force.

Damn….

Chapter 8

DEX WAS exhausted. The last week had been busy, and yet not busy enough. After Sunday he hadn't seen Les at all and their texts had grown fewer and father between. The store was taking all his time, and he was trying to get his legs under him. At the same time, he wondered if maybe he was spending too much time working, as things with Les seemed to cool some and Dex didn't quite know why.

Unfortunately, so far his hard work wasn't exactly paying off. On Wednesday he took in a total of a hundred dollars. Thankfully the other days had been a bit better and he had been able to get in some of the books his customers had requested. Sales picked up at the end of the week, and he got a quick message from Les, which he hadn't seen for an hour because he'd been busy at the time. Still, if he couldn't build up more business, he was going to be out on his butt.

At least Julio had been good enough to arrange to have his stuff packed and shipped. "Consider it your goodbye present," he'd said with a smile through Skype. "I wish things had worked out, but family is… well, family."

"Thank you."

"They're shipping your car too. I got you a deal." He grinned, and Dex wondered what that meant. "All costs are covered. Don't worry about a thing."

Julio's phone had rung in the background, and he had said goodbye. Dex's screen went blank and that was it. His old life was gone, just like that.

Dex closed his computer and looked up at his empty bookstore, wondering if he was trading his failed dream in for his mother's. He turned, looking out the windows and up toward Les's apartment, wondering if he should call him. He made a mental note to talk after work. But the bell above the door tinkled, pulling him out of his wonderings. People came in, and with a sigh, he went into customer service mode.

SATURDAY WAS a zoo in the very best way possible. Dex had put up signs and saturated the store's limited social media with news of a children's reading group. Jane agreed to work the register for part of the day, so Dex brought the most colorful clothes he had with him, including a wild plaid bow tie that had been his dad's, and acted out Babar. He had changed in his mother's Alice in Wonderland bathroom, looking a little like a character from the story himself.

"Are you ready?" Dex asked as he stepped out of the back room to a group of jumping, happy kids, who laughed and clapped when they saw him. Dex looked around the room and caught Les's gaze from where he stood about halfway back. God, it was so good just to see his smile. The nerves that had built in his stomach dissipated in seconds, and he picked up the book and began to read.

As soon as he began, it was like he was on stage, and he let himself get into what he was going. He did Babar's voice and Celeste's, as well as the other characters, making the kids laugh and clap. Even the parents seemed to be having a good time as they stood nearby, listening and hopefully browsing.

The kids cheered when he read the last line. Then he pulled out his copy of Madeline and read that as well. He wanted to make sure that he read stories with boy and girl main characters. When he was done, he took an exaggerated bow and the reading group broke up, the kids hurrying back to their parents, hopefully to beg for books. Which, of course, was the whole point of story time.

"That was awesome." Les smiled as Dex helped Jane ring up purchases. "Have you eaten?"

"Not really," Dex said before returning his attention to one of the mothers. She had a stack of books for herself and her daughter.

"I just love that you do this. I've been trying to get Gwen to read herself, and she's always wanting me to read to her. I'm hoping that the books will encourage her."

Dex leaned over the counter. "My mom read to me until I was almost ten—we loved spending that time together. Sometimes my dad joined us." Dex hurried out to one of the aisles and brought back a copy of The Lion, the Witch, and the Wardrobe. "This was the last book that all three of us read together. We took turns by chapter, but my dad read all the Aslan parts in his deep, booming voice."

She smiled and nodded. "You've really given me something to think about. Maybe taking turns is the answer." Her smile burned bright, and Dex bagged all the books, then said goodbye as other people entered the store.

"Wow," Dex breathed.

"I'd say that was a success," Jane said.

"Yes. Next week I need to read a story that's a little longer for some of the slightly older kids." He breathed a sigh and met Les as he came over.

"Do you want to get some dinner after closing?"

Dex grinned. "Oh God, yes." He missed Les and hated that he had been so busy all week that he hadn't had much time for anything other than the store. Dex was starting to understand that this was going to be his life for a while.

He spent the rest of the late afternoon with customers. Finally, as evening approached, the flow of customers slowed. Dex checked the time and started going through some of his cleanup procedures so he wouldn't have to do it later.

"Why don't you two go on to dinner?" Jane suggested.

"That would be great. Thanks. Just let me take care of the deposit. Les and I can drop it off. Then all you'll need to do is put the rest in the safe." Dex went in back and prepped the deposit. "Are you sure about this?"

Jane rolled her eyes. "I've been closing this store for years for Sarah. I can do it for you. Just go and have a good time. If I need anything, you'll be at Molly Pitcher's, right?"

"Yes," Dex answered.

"Just go before you drive me crazy." She smiled and shooed them out of the store.

Dex walked slowly, keeping pace with Les for the short trip to the bank and then the taproom.

"Why are you so quiet?" Dex asked before they reached their destination. Traffic and the associated headlights created a visual distraction and audible din that was difficult to speak over.

"I'm not," Les answered, but Dex knew it was a lie. Something was different; he just didn't know what it was. Yes, he had been busy, but for the past week, Les's texts and even the way they'd spoken on the phone had seemed more distant. Dex could almost feel a space opening up between them. Even now, with Les right next to him, it was as if an unnamed someone walked between them.

"Les, have I done something?" Dex didn't dare to take his hand for fear he would be rejected. Why, he wasn't sure, but the notion was there, and it wouldn't go away.

"No," Les answered without pausing in his steps. "Why?"

Dex was the one to stop. "You aren't talking, and you usually have plenty to say. I have barely seen you in a week, and when we talk, you only answer questions. It's been strange, and I don't know why." He kept trying to go over it. "Is your foot okay? Are you in pain? Do you not want to see me any longer? Is that what this is about? Maybe you think I'm boring and I work too hard? Am I terrible in bed?" That last one he added as a sort of joke, and at least Les smiled.

"No. You're definitely good in bed. After all, I can't seem to let you out of it once we're together." But he gave no further explanation, which only made Dex wonder more.

"Is that all?"

"I don't know what you want from me," Les said.

"Excuse me? Want from you? I don't want anything from you other than the truth. What's going on? Is there something wrong?" He caught Les's gaze and found the same intensity and touch of softness his eyes had always held, and as he watched, they grew gentler. Something was very off, but Dex had no idea what. That bothered him.

"There's…. I don't know what it is you want from us, from this. What's between us," Les told him.

"What do you mean? I want what we want. Do you not want to see if there's something real going on?" Dex took Les's hand, letting go of his fear because he needed a connection, something that would make Les seem a little closer. "What is it you want?"

"Honesty and openness," Les answered softly. "I want things to be good, and I want to protect you from what could hurt you, but you have to let me. I need to know that you and I feel the same way about certain things." He didn't pull his hand away.

"What sort of things?" Dex asked. "I really don't know what you're talking about."

Les's jaw clenched and his gaze grew harder. "Look. I don't know what was going on with the store before you got it, but…." He inhaled sharply. "But I need to know if you have found anything that might shed any light on what your mother might have been doing. You have to tell me or I can't protect you."

Dex held Les's gaze right back, wondering if he should come clean about what he'd found. Let Les take care of it and have it over with. But he wasn't sure what would happen if anyone found out. Would they try to close the store? Hell, the accounts for the store would be called into question, as would his mother's income. A million things went through his mind in a split second. "What do you want me to tell you?"

"The truth," Les said.

Dex glanced around. "That I run a bookstore that was my mother's?"

Les took a small step closer. "No. I want to know how your mother kept the store running all those years. I see what you're doing. There are days when only three for four people come in. How can you make a living that way? And your mom didn't do any more business than you are. Most of the time, it was less."

Dex nodded. "Then come with me." He continued up the sidewalk, passed the taproom, and continued up to the corner. He turned right with Les behind him and then once again, down the alley that led behind the store, where he unlocked the back door.

The building was quiet. Jane had already closed and locked up. Dex grabbed one of the books and handed it to Les. "Yes, I know." Les sniffed it. "I know what this contained at one point. I can still smell the remnants of it. What I want to know is who your mother was selling it to and where she was getting the stuff."

Dex sighed and pulled the plastic-bag-wrapped box out from under the shelf. "I found this as I was going through things back here. Most of these books have a small amount inside them in plastic bags. And to answer your question, I don't know where Mom was getting it."

"But she was a pot dealer? A drug pusher?" His eyes blazed. "Nothing more?"

Dex's frustration rose and he pushed the box against Les's chest. "Mom was selling pot, but she wasn't dealing. Not in the way your ratlike mind seems to think." Les flinched, but Dex didn't care. "I take it you had been watching the store from your window on the other side the street. Yeah, you kept the curtains closed when I was there, but I'm not dumb. Now it all makes sense. Did you try to get close to me so you could find this out? Because if you did, you'll be disappointed. I haven't done anything with any of it. I just wrapped it up and stuck it where I got it from."

Les held the box, his cane dropping to the floor. Dex picked it up and set it on the nearby table. "What do you expect me to do with this?"

"I don't know. You seem to think you have all the answers, so I figured I'd dump this little problem in your hands. You handle it from now on. Oh, but don't think about the fact that it will be the end of my business. Who will bring their family here for story time if they find out? You know there's no way the business can survive this." He leaned against the table. "So you do whatever you think you need to."

Les didn't say anything right away. "I'm a police officer. Or I was. I can't just turn a blind eye to someone selling drugs. Who knows who she was selling them to and what harm came to any of them?"

Dex rolled his eyes. "Right. I'd say you don't know as much as you think you do."

"Please. Kids could have gotten their hands on this. Who knows how many…?"

"Hold it, Mr. High-and-Mighty. I know who Mom's customers were… and they weren't kids."

"Excuse me?" Les said, still holding the plastic-encased box.

"You heard me. Mom's customers weren't kids. They were little old ladies."

Les smiled and then laughed nervously. "Right."

"I'm serious," Dex snapped. "Do you know anything about medical marijuana? Probably not, since you're too busy being a pain in the ass. It's a real thing, and it helps a number of conditions, including nausea, joint pain, and severe insomnia, among others. Here, in this backward state, you have to jump through more hoops than a trained lion in order to get it. Mom's customers were crippled little old ladies who could barely move because their arthritis is so bad. I met a lot of them, and I nearly went ahead and gave them the stuff just because of how desperate they are. These are people who only wanted some relief from chronic pain for a few hours, to just be able to move joints that are usually so swollen that they're stiff."

Les's expression softened. "How do you know this?"

"Because one of Mom's customers told me. She had to be nearing ninety, and it was obvious she was in constant pain. You should understand better than most what that's like, and how good a few hours' relief actually feels." He glared at Les, who set the box on the table.

"You're telling me that your mom...."

"Was trying to provide a service to people—one that the state isn't willing to. It's really stupid. There are a few dispensaries in Philadelphia, but that doesn't help anyone around here." Dex picked up the box and slipped it under the shelf once more. "I haven't sold any of it and I don't know what to do with the stuff, but my mom was trying to help others. That I know for certain."

"Are you sure?" Les pressed.

"I'm just as sure about my mom as I am that you are being a real ass. Maybe I should just go home and make my own dinner. You can call your cop friends. You know where the stuff is. I'm not going to move it." He was breathing as though he had run a marathon. "You follow your conscience and do what you think is best." Dex folded his arms over his chest, staring at Les.

Les's stance softened and he sighed. "You never sold any of it."

Dex shook his head. "No, I didn't. But that doesn't mean I wasn't tempted. I had days where I made next to nothing. I could have, but that wasn't how I wanted to make the business work. Even though one of Mom's customers explained why she had done it, I've played it down and made believe I didn't know what they were asking for.

I think word is getting around, because they aren't asking nearly as often. And before you ask, I'm not giving you any of the details. That part of the business's history needs to be in the past. I have to figure out how to make the business work without it." He had said what he needed to. "I think we're done here. If you had suspicions and wanted to find out what was going on, you've accomplished that. Your hunch was right. Now I think you can go. I'll let you out the front door, and you can go back to your apartment satisfied." He headed toward the sales floor.

"Wait," Les said softly. "I didn't start seeing you because I was suspicious. Yeah, I thought that something was going on, but I never dreamed it was this, and I certainly didn't date you to discover out what it was." Dex turned, and Les stood, leaning on his cane with one hand and using the doorframe for support with the other.

"Is that why you stayed away all week?" Dex asked.

Les nodded. "I was getting closer to you, and I couldn't keep my suspicions from taking over my thoughts. And then when we were here, I found one of the hollowed-out books, and it smelled like…. Well, I think you get the idea. I knew that I had been right, but I couldn't figure out what to do about it."

Dex's throat hurt. He just wanted to go back to the house, crawl into his old bed, and try to forget all about it. "So you…."

"I asked, dammit. I didn't call the police and have them raid the place. I knew, and yet I asked you. Doesn't that count for something?" He seemed so vulnerable—something Dex knew damned well that Les hated more than anything. Still, it hurt that someone he cared about had suspected him of wrongdoing. "Do you know what that took for me? My instincts were to turn in what I'd found and have the police handle it. That was what I had been trained to do. But I didn't. I waited and asked you about it." Les almost shook with tension.

If Dex was honest with himself, the reason he hadn't said anything to Les was because he hadn't been sure how Les would react. "I…."

"You didn't say anything about what you'd found." Les's voice held disappointment, and Dex hated that sound.

"Because I was afraid of what you'd think," Dex said honestly. "I know how you feel about this sort of thing, and I didn't know what to do with what I had found. So I packed it away and hid it until I could figure it out." He felt his defiance deflating. "I just couldn't figure out what in the hell I was going to do. I could have sold the stuff and just let that be the end of it. There's enough there to bring in a thousand dollars, I think. But that wasn't how I wanted to finance my store." He sighed. "I was tempted. That money would have bought quite a bit of new stock that I could have used to keep the store fresh. And I think that was what Mom was doing. Over and over again. I was so stupid. I thought that if I just stocked the right things, people would come in for them. But the issue here, with this store, is more fundamental—people don't think about the store anymore."

Les got the box and put it on the table. "What do you want to do with this?"

"I don't know what to do. I want it to disappear. But I can't burn it or just toss it into the trash. Whatever Mom was doing needs to end."

"Then just flush the stuff. That's easy enough. The evidence will be gone and you can throw away the books." Les stayed where he was.

Dex took a step closer to him. "But there's more. What can I do about the people who need help? These poor folks are in pain. I can't just turn my back on them."

Les sighed. "I understand. But this is a schedule-one controlled substance, like it or not. Some states have legalized it, but that doesn't change the fact that the federal government still considers it illegal. As for the people who need it, the best way to do anything is to work with the state to get them what they need. But right now this is more than you and I can fix." He turned away from the table and picked up his cane, heading for the back door.

"Where are you going?" Dex asked. He felt the distance building between them.

He paused. "I need to...."

"Help me get rid of this stuff," Dex interjected as he reached for the plastic bag that encased the box.

Les shook his head. "I can't. You're asking me to help you destroy evidence."

"Of a crime committed by someone who is dead. What I'm asking you to do is to help put an end to it. I had nothing to do with this, and yet I could be the one to pay for my mom's little side venture with everything I have left." Dex released the box and left it where it was. "Maybe that's not such a bad idea. I can let the store go before it sinks me too. Maybe have a sale and clear out the inventory. Then I can rent out the retail space and live in my tiny apartment. I can get a job waiting tables, because it's about the only thing I'm qualified for, and spend the rest of my life living with half a dozen cats."

"Cats?" Les asked, the hint of a smile around his lips. "Really? You're trying to make me feel guilty with cats?"

"I figured you were a dog kind of guy, so yeah, cats."

Les rolled his eyes. "Come on. Let's take care of this stuff so we can go get something to eat."

"You're really going to help me?" Dex asked as Les picked up the box from the table.

"You're right. This isn't going to do anyone anything but harm. And if I want to keep you out of trouble—which I'm beginning to think could end up being a full-time job—then we need to get this done. Then we can finally eat before my stomach starts to think my throat has been cut." He carried the box toward the bathroom, pulled it out of the plastic, and began opening the books inside. Les handed Dex the first of the little plastic bags, and he dumped the contents into the toilet.

"You know, doing this gives a whole new meaning to the term 'down the rabbit hole,' doesn't it?" Dex asked, glancing at the cartoon of Alice.

Les snorted slightly. "We can think of it as flushing Wonderland."

THE LAST of what they found in the box of hollowed-out books was gone, and Dex could finally breathe a little easier. They placed all the books as well as the bags in the large plastic bag, and after the two of the left the store via the back door, Dex dropped it in one of the dumpsters down the way as they walked around toward the front of the building.

Thunder sounded in the distance, and by the time they got to the door of the taproom, the rain had started. Dex stood in the doorway, watching as the rain pelted the street and sidewalk. He was tempted to step out into it—let the rain wash everything away. He had a chance at a new start, and the past—his past—was gone. It was time to look forward.

"Are you coming inside?" Les asked. "You're getting wet."

Dex turned around and went into the restaurant.

"You're acting strange," Les told him.

"I know." He smiled. "I guess I'm relieved." They found an empty table near the windows, and Dex sat down and leaned across the table. "I hated keeping that from you, and I spent the last week wondering what to do with it. Every time I came into the store, I looked at that shelf... every single time." He sighed. "I can't help wondering how Mom got into that business in the first place."

The server came to their table, and Dex ordered the chicken sandwich without looking at the menu. He was too intent on Les to even think. It was hard for him to comprehend that whatever his mother had started was over and that Les had helped him.

Les ordered as well, and the server left the table. "Who knows? I knew your mom and I never thought badly of her. I still don't." He leaned closer. "But I'm worried. She had to have a supplier somewhere."

Dex nodded. "I thought of that too. It's part of the reason I kept it—in case someone came asking for payment or something." He had no idea how things like this worked.

Les snickered. "I'm pretty sure those guys don't take returns."

Dex had figured as much. "But I had no idea if there was something outstanding. The last thing I needed was for someone to break into the store or something like they do in the movies. And I like my legs in one piece."

"Now you're being a little silly. These guys don't take credit—everything is cash—so your mom paid for her inventory up front." Les rolled his eyes. "It took some courage and strength of character for you to do what you just did."

Dex took Les's hand. "I want the store to be a success, but I won't do it that way. I want to make it work on my own. But one thing is becoming very clear—I'm going to need to find a way to make some money in order for that to happen. This store isn't going to be able to make it simply by selling books. Not today. When Mom and Dad started the store, the world was different. Amazon didn't exist, so books had to be bought locally. Now there are e-books, and you can order any paperback or hardcover you want and have it delivered to your home." He paused and scratched his head. "If I want people to come into the store regularly, I'm going to have to do something different. Sure, I can create reading groups and book clubs, but there has to be something else. Coffee has been done, and the store isn't big enough for a café anyway. But it doesn't matter—I don't have the money to do any of it."

"I see," Les said softly.

"You have no idea how tempting it was to just…." He didn't even want to say it in so public a place, but with a nod, Les seemed to understand. "I'm sorry if I put you in a bad position."

"No, I get it. If you hadn't told me, then…." He seemed to be probing for some answer.

"I would have figured out a way to get rid of it. But then you wouldn't be conflicted, and don't tell me that you weren't. I can see it in your eyes." He wished that none of this had happened. "But at least it's over… I hope." God, he sure as hell hoped there were no more surprises in store.

"I think I understand," Les told him. "I can even understand why you want to help those people…." The server brought their beers, and he paused until she had left again. "The ones your mom was trying to aid. But there isn't anything you can do, and getting on the wrong side of the law could cost you everything."

Dex was aware of that. But he had to do something. He just had to figure out what. "I'm not going to say who they are. I won't. These are good people." He wasn't going to make more hassles for them.

"Okay. That I understand. But what about the source? What if you find that out?" Les seemed so intense.

"If I find out who they are, I'll call you right away," Dex promised. "Though I suspect that particular avenue died along with Mom. At least I hope it did. No one has come into the store trying to sell me something, at least."

Les nodded and smiled. "Then we're good." He squeezed Dex's hand, and most of the tension in Les's eyes slipped away, replaced by the same intensity that had drawn Dex to him the first time he'd seen the man. "Do you want to come over to my place after we eat? I have a few movies we can watch."

Dex breathed a sigh of relief. "I was hoping you'd offer." The past week had had him wondering if he had somehow blown things with Les. But he now realized being up front with him had been the right decision. Dex hoped he would always be able to do that.

Their food arrived, and Dex ate his amazingly crunchy and spicy chicken sandwich, savoring every bite, even as his gaze rarely left Les and the way he slowly chewed his food. Who would've thought eating could be sexy, but it seemed to Dex that the more he watched, the more he realized that just about everything Les did was sexy. It made him wish their dinner was over so he and Les could get to what he hoped would be the intimately special part of the evening.

"Hey, Les, how are you doing?" a man said when he approached the table.

"I'm good. I don't think you've met Dex. This is my friend Red." They shook hands. "What brings you over?" Les tensed at his own question.

"I was going to call you when I got home tonight." Red glanced at Dex and then back to Les. "I found something, but I'm not sure what to make of it."

Dex put down his sandwich and excused himself.

He had this feeling in the pit of his stomach that he knew what the conversation would be about. It was best that he let the two of them talk. He went to the bathroom and used the facilities, then washed his hands.

When he returned, Red and Les were still talking softly, with Red leaning far over the table. Their gazes were intense, and Les was paler than he'd been when Dex had left. Once Dex got back to his seat, he glanced at the two men. "Is everything okay?"

Les shook his head. "It seems you might have been right about my former partner. I talked to Red earlier this week, and he said he'd look into things." He slowly released his breath.

"I don't have anything concrete on Williams, but I asked some of the guys who were on the scene about it. They said that Williams's story didn't quite add up, but no one was able to offer anything to contradict him." Red rubbed the back of his neck. "I wish I had more for you. But...."

Les lowered his gaze to the table. "I guess I had hoped that someone might have seen something more solid. Then again, it would've been a long shot." The betrayal in Les's eyes made Dex want to hunt this Williams guy down. If he hurt Les or purposely allowed Les to get hurt, he deserved to have his nuts removed and used as ping-pong balls.

"I'll keep my eyes and ears open. A few of my friends are going to see if they can rattle Williams's cage. We may only suspect something, but we can play it up a little and see if he cracks." Red patted Les's shoulder. "Most of the guys aren't really happy with him."

"I see." Les was so subdued. After the fire Dex had seen in his eyes earlier, this was quite a contrast.

Red glanced at him. "Did anything come of what we spoke about?"

Les sighed. "Yes and no. It isn't something we need to worry about right now. The issue is in the past, and no good can come of it. Besides, it wasn't at all what I thought. Maybe we can share the story over a drink sometime." Dex figured Les had mentioned his suspicions regarding his mom to Red. "But if anything comes up, we'll definitely let you know."

Red nodded. "Good enough. I'll be in touch if I have anything, and the same goes for you." He left the table.

Dex released the breath he'd been holding. "I take it you shared your suspicions with him." He wasn't sure how he felt about that.

"Yeah. He thought I was probably imagining things. He did say that your mom's store wasn't on anyone's radar. But like I told him, it's over—at least as far as I'm concerned—and Red isn't going to take it any further. He has plenty to do on his own. There's nothing to be gained by anyone looking into it now," Les said, finishing the last of his sandwich.

Dex, on the other hand, wasn't hungry any longer. "But what about your old partner? What are we going to do? We can't let him get away with this."

"First thing, there isn't anything that we can do. I have to let Red and the others do their jobs. If I get involved, then Williams is going to know that something is up. He'll tighten his story and we'll never find out a thing. As much as I want to hang the guy out to dry by his ears, I have to sit back and let the others take the lead." Les drummed his fingers on the tabletop.

"I take it you hate that idea as much as I do," Dex said, gently silencing Les's fingers. "Are you done?"

Les nodded. "Finish your dinner and we'll get going."

Dex ate the rest of the food without really tasting it, and Les paid the check. The rain had stopped, and the two of them walked across the water-slicked street and over to Les's upstairs apartment and went inside.

"I have to ask something, and you can tell me to shut up if you want. I won't be offended." Dex pulled Les into his arms, hoping to provide some sort of comfort. Red's news had to have rocked Les's world. "If your partner was involved… why would he do that? Regardless of whether he liked you or not, why would he just stay back like that? It's a huge risk…. The suspects could have talked, you could have seen something…. I can't help feeling there has to be more."

Les lifted his gaze. "Unless he knew the suspects would never talk."

"Yeah. I mean, we know the guy is bad. He has to be, to act that way. A normal person doesn't just let someone get hurt if they can stop it…." He let his words trail off. Dex was probably opening a can of worms that would lead nowhere.

"No. You're right." Les pulled out his phone and texted like crazy for a few minutes.

"Anything?"

"Red said he's going to look into it but has to be careful." Les set the phone aside. "I'm not sure what he can do, at least without tipping his hand, but he'll try."

"So he agrees that it's possible Williams is dirty. But we don't know what kind of dirt," Dex said, thinking about the scripts he'd read, but Les put up his hands to stop him.

"We need to try to figure this out. We don't have enough information to do anything about this right now, and if we were to try to get it like they do on television, then…." He guided Dex toward the bedroom. "Well, this isn't the movies. If Williams did nothing to help me on purpose…." Les breathed deeply, and Dex could feel the tension in his body. Each step for Les seemed halting, as if his knees wouldn't bend properly. "If he actually acted that way, then the guy is dangerous and doesn't give a shit about anything. He wouldn't think twice about hurting either of us, and there are many things I can do, but…." Les looked downward. "I don't think I'm up to being anyone's hero anymore."

Chapter 9

AND THERE it was, the frankest admission he'd ever made in his life. In one sentence, Les had nearly laid his soul bare for Dex. He wanted to go to his room, crawl under the covers, and hide for the next twenty years.

"Come on," Dex said softly, and Les figured he was pretending not to have heard. At least Dex didn't say something ridiculous, like he would "always be a hero" or "there's nothing wrong with you." Maybe something even worse, like "you're perfect just the way you are." If he had, Les probably would have kicked him out of the apartment and willed Dex into that special level of hell that only existed for people who dished out platitudes.

"Dex...." He sighed. "I...." The need to be alone almost overwhelmed him. Maybe a damned hole would open up and he'd never be seen again. Les rolled his eyes at his own thoughts.

"Come to bed," Dex whispered, his voice as enticing as a buffet to a starving man. He said nothing more than that, but instead guided them toward the room and then closed the door behind them. Only the light from around the curtains illuminated the bare outline of the room. It was enough. The air conditioner hummed softly, cooling the room. Dex got him to the bed, and Les sat down, glad to be off his feet but embarrassed and feeling useless. What the hell was he good for? "Les." Dex tapped his leg, and he lifted his foot.

Dex removed Les's shoes and then placed his hands on his knees, parting them before moving between them. He pressed right to Les, smoothing his hands over Les's head and down to his neck and back. Thank God Dex kept quiet. It gave Les the chance to sink into his own head and away from the reality of the remnants of his life for just a few seconds.

Then Dex kissed him right at the base of his neck, those hot, sweet lips moving upward, to behind his ear. Les closed his eyes and tried to fight it, but within moments he stretched his neck, giving Dex what he wanted.

Dex pressed Les back on the bed, unfastening the buttons of his shirt, letting the fabric fall to both sides of his body. The cool air kissed his hot skin, and Les let out a sigh he couldn't hold in any longer.

Dex kissed down his chest, sliding his hands along behind his lips, only adding to the heat of the trail he blazed. He said nothing, which had Les wondering what was going through his mind. Dex's hands were all the expression that was necessary, and Les knew what he wanted just by the simplest touch. When he rested his hand on his shoulder, Les shrugged out of his shirt, and as he ran them down his side, Les quivered with anticipation. And when he unfastened Les's belt and his pants, he lifted his hips, and soon the last of his clothing slipped off his legs.

For a few seconds, Les wondered if he should be self-conscious under Dex's intense gaze. But there was no time. Dex guided him up toward the pillows and then stood next to the bed, slowly removing his own clothes. He turned around so all Les saw was the outline of a strong back and arms flexing as muscles bunched and then elongated when Dex pulled his shirt over his head. God, that was a beautiful sight.

One thunk followed another as Dex kicked off his shoes, and then, still facing away from Les, Dex rocked his hips from side to side, back elongating until the twin half globes of his incredible ass made an appearance. Les swallowed to wet his lips and suddenly dry throat. He groaned, longing to touch, to taste. But Dex stayed just out of reach, and still, he said nothing.

Dex turned slowly, giving him the view of a hip and then a strong leg bent forward just enough to entice. He paused and then continued until he faced Les in all his strong, masculine glory. Dex stood still, letting Les look his fill, before closing the distance between them.

"What are you playing at?" Les asked with a smile, but he received only a crook of the lips in return. "Is this the silent treatment?"

"No. This is the 'sometimes we talk way too damn much' treatment." Dex placed his finger over Les's lips. "You can make any sound you like as long as it's a moan, groan, whimper, or cry of passion.

Otherwise, just let yourself go." He captured Les's lips before he could argue, and Les wound his hand around to the back of Dex's neck, caressing his hair as their kiss deepened and Les forgot about what was weighing him down.

Les moaned softly into Dex's lips, loving the taste and the heat. Without breaking contact, Dex maneuvered himself onto the bed, pressing Les into the mattress. Dex was right—there was no need for words. They could communicate what they wanted in so many more delightful ways.

Dex groaned deeply as Les wound his fingers around his cock, stroking slowly, loving the way Dex shivered against him, driving the excitement between them. Les lifted his legs, signaling exactly what he wanted from Dex, and damned if he didn't groan once again.

"I want you to roll over," Dex whispered. "I know I'm breaking my own rule about silence, but I won't take any chances on hurting you." He backed away, and Les slowly rolled onto his belly. Dex's warm hands caressed his foot, and Les closed his eyes, sighing as the tension left his muscles. Sometimes he would give anything to make the discomfort stop, and Dex seemed to be able to make that happen with just a simple touch. He groaned as Dex slid his hands up his legs, caressing his thighs and then his butt, working the muscles as though he were kneading dough—slowly, fluidly, and with just enough pressure to send chills racing up Les's spine to his brain, where they scrambled his thoughts.

Les gripped the edges of the mattress and let himself go. Putting himself in Dex's hands was easy. Trust was difficult sometimes, especially when it came to his foot, and yet he willingly let Dex take control. It seemed so natural that he barely gave it any thought, even as Dex ghosted a finger over his entrance. One became two, and then Dex teased the skin behind his balls, sending a wave of desire through him.

Dex seemed to be able to break down his walls without even trying. Les spread his legs farther, moaning softly while Dex's hands worked their magic. Then they pulled away, and Les lifted his head to see what was going on.

"Holy hell!" Les cried as wet heat pressed to his skin. "What are you…?"

He arched his back and growled as Dex teased the flesh around his opening, tongue and fingers working together until Les gasped for breath, his mouth hanging open as wave after wave of sensation flowed through him, each building on the next until it all became too much. He wanted to tell Dex to stop, to give him a chance to inhale, but damned if he was going to interrupt this joyride to heaven that Dex was taking him on. Fucking hell, he'd had no idea this existed. Les had never trusted anyone enough to let them put him in the bottom role, yet here, Dex was showing him just what heights he could be driven to.

"What do you want, Les?" Dex asked, trailing his tongue up Les's back to his shoulder before kissing him hard. "You need to tell me what it is you want from me."

"You… all of you." Les's brain short-circuited completely. "Just you." He closed his eyes as Dex shifted behind him. He heard a tear of foil and then felt some cool lube slicking him. Finally Dex's magic fingers returned. He quivered through preparation, and then Dex pressed to him, slowly sliding inside, filling him.

Les gasped, and Dex stopped, sliding a hand around his chest, holding him closer as he slowly sank deeper inside him. This was incredible and exactly what Les wanted. The stretch, the burn, followed by a heady, deep warmth that smoothed the way and gave him the intimacy he craved. Dex paused and sucked his ear, holding him close, just the two of them together. Les pressed back against Dex as a signal, but Dex stayed right there, moving slowly, staying close.

Dex moved long and slow, pulling each and every ounce of passion out of Les. There was no drive to the end zone. This was a gradual buildup until Les's head pounded and he begged for release. But Dex kept up his steady pace until Les's eyes rolled back into his head and he could take no more, careening off the precipice of desire in a flying leap that left him breathless.

"Are you okay?" Dex asked when their bodies disconnected. "I didn't hurt you, did I?"

Les rolled over and tugged Dex down to him. "No. You were perfect." He buried his face in Dex's shoulder and just held him. After that kind of vulnerability, he needed a few seconds to get himself together, and he didn't want Dex to see him come apart.

"It's okay," Dex whispered, holding him.

"I don't know what's wrong with me." He had never gone to pieces like this after sex. Yes, he had been vulnerable before, but never to this extent. It was not just physically, but emotionally. He had opened himself up to Dex, and now he needed to figure out a way to close the door, or at least stop Dex from seeing him so intensely all the time.

"It's difficult letting someone else see that part of you. You can tell people your stories and share parts of yourself, but in those moments, you choose what to share." Dex nuzzled his neck. "You have nothing to be worried about. Whatever you show me when we're alone will stay between us. I promise you that."

Les sighed. He already knew that. Not in his mind, but in his heart. But he still needed a few minutes. "Thank you."

"For what?"

"Everything—for being here… for…." He didn't even know what he was trying to say, so he just gave up. It wasn't necessary.

Dex took care of the condom and then settled next to him, and Les sighed as he shifted closer. He closed his eyes and smiled. "I love this."

"The time for just the two of us?"

Les hummed softly. "Yeah." He tugged Dex nearer. "Do you want to talk or something?"

"If you want to," Dex offered.

Les rolled his head from side to side on the pillow. There were times when being quiet was preferable, and this was one of those for him.

As if realizing this, Dex said, "Why don't you close your eyes and go to sleep."

Les nodded and tried to get his restless mind to quiet.

Chapter 10

DEX SAT behind the counter, staring out at a store empty of customers. Not a single one. It had been that way for almost the entire day.

He kept telling himself not to worry and to get other things done. He had a list of tasks to complete, so he pushed himself out of the mopes and got to work. Since it was slow, he decided to rearrange some of the shelves. By moving a few and more creatively using the space, he thought he might be able to enlarge the reading area and bring in another chair to encourage people to linger. He'd brought in a coffee pot and had begun offering free coffee to customers in the hope that they might take a seat and hang around a little. It might work… if anyone bothered to come through the door in the first place.

He was just finishing up when the bell on the door jingled. "Hello," Dex said as a man in his early twenties, dressed in a polo shirt and jeans, wandered into the store. "Feel free to browse." He finished replacing the books on the shelf, keeping an eye on the customer in case he needed anything. Once he was done, Dex returned to the counter and organized the already perfect supplies just to try to keep himself busy.

"I'm glad the store is still open," the young man said. Dex straightened up. "You're Sarah's son, right? I liked her. She was a nice lady and a good customer." He smiled, perfect teeth shining.

A chill went down Dex's spine. "A customer of yours?" Dex asked, thinking it best to play dumb.

He grinned and leaned on the counter. "Of course." He seemed completely at ease, while Dex was afraid he'd sweat through his shirt in about thirty seconds. "I'm sure you've been through everything in the store, so you probably know about her little side business." The man's gaze was as sharp as broken glass. Dex used all his acting skills to keep his expression neutral. "There's no need to be coy. I know you know what she was doing, and since the police haven't been swarming the place, I also know you haven't called them. Did you figure out the system to keep the ladies flying high?" He smiled at his own joke.

Dex swallowed but didn't answer.

"I'm not here to shake you down or anything. Geez. I'm just the guy who grew what she sold. I'm not going to squeal or anything. I'll have some new product ready in a few days. Should I bring it by?"

"Is this something you do... like, professionally?"

He shook his head. "God, no. I'm just trying to pay for college. I have a secret location where I grow some plants. Nothing more." He snorted in a very undignified manner, and Dex could now see just how young he really was.

"How did you get started with this sort of thing?" Dex asked, trying to gather some information. Up until now, Dex hadn't done anything wrong, and he had no intention of starting. But information was power. He wished he could get Les down here to talk to this guy.

"Well, honestly, I've grown a plant or two for a long time. My gran had bad arthritis, and when I gave her some, it helped her a lot." He smiled. "Can you imagine smoking a joint with your grandma? She only took a few puffs. It didn't take much for her, but it sure helped. And before she died, Gran told me about your mom." The deep loss that darkened his eyes was real, as far as Dex could see. He'd witnessed plenty of bad acting, and this wasn't it. "The store needed a little extra cash flow, and there are plenty of people like my gran who couldn't get the help they needed."

Dex sighed. "You make it sound like you were providing a service."

"I am. Duh. The laws here are ridiculous, and those people needed help. Even a policeman friend of mine says so. I make a little extra money so I can get through college without being swamped in debt, your mom made some extra cash, and the people who needed help got it." He shrugged in a big way, like the kid he was. "We aren't hurting anyone."

Dex wasn't going to argue that, but he couldn't seem to get past the mention of the kid's "policeman friend" and just what was going on there. Though he doubted he'd get details. Whether they thought they laws were wrong or not, this kid and his friend had hurt him and the memory of his mother. Yeah, knowing her, she had done this for the right reasons. She never hesitated to help people. But their little scheme had turned his mom into a drug dealer and the business he was trying to save into a front for illegal activity.

The front door opened and a pair of ladies with their young daughters came in and headed right for the children's section. "It's still here!" one of the girls said a little loudly, but with ringing joy.

"Excuse me a moment, will you?" Dex wandered over to the children's area to see if his new customers needed help. He passed behind the low shelves that ran through the center of the store and pulled out his phone, sending a text to Les to get over there. He dropped the phone in his pocket as he approached the women. They apparently needed no assistance, so he returned to the counter while his guest wandered the store. It seemed that whatever his visitor had to say, he wanted to do privately.

The doorbell tinkled as Les entered the store, leaning on his cane. Dex's first thought was to wonder if he was hurting. "Can I help you, sir?" Dex asked, hoping Les would pick up on his cue.

Les slowly approached the desk. "Do you have the latest John Grisham?"

Dex breathed a sigh of relief—Les understood the situation—then got the book.

"The guy Mom dealt with is by the door," Dex said quietly. Then, louder, he added, "I love this book. He really gets into the action." He set the book aside. "Is that all you wanted?"

"Let me look around." Les moved away as the girls brought up four books each and the mothers two.

Dex rang up the sales for each woman. "Those are wonderful. Are you interested in our Saturday afternoon reading hour?" He handed them each a brochure. "I do all the voices myself. It's a lot of fun." He finished wrapping the books, then handed over the bags. "Thank you."

"Bye," the girls said in unison as they skipped to the door.

Dex followed them, then flipped the sign to Closed on the door.

"Okay," Les said, turning to the young visitor. "I think you and I need to have a talk."

"Who are you?" The kid's cockiness was interesting.

"I'm a police officer on leave, and Dex here is my boyfriend."
Les closed his arms over his chest as Dex's visitor paled.

"Les, just listen to what he has to say," Dex said, trying to
calm him.

"Let's start with your name," Les said.

"You can call me Peter." The kid crossed his arms over his chest
as well. "If you're on leave, then you aren't on duty. I want to leave
right now."

"I could call my friends and they'd be here in minutes. Before
you even got out the door, they'd have your picture and know
everything you told Dex. So if you're smart, you'll tell me what I
want to know. And by the way…" He smiled. "…Sarah's little side
business is over."

Pete's shoulders slumped, and he gave Les the same story he'd
told Dex. "I don't grow it for anyone else. As a cop, you have to know
how hard it is for people who need marijuana to get it. My grandmother
needed it. And so do the people Sarah and I were helping." He shook
now, his confidence long gone.

"You said something about a police officer?" Dex prompted,
figuring now was as good a time as any to finally get some answers.

Peter nodded. "Yeah. After about six months of working with
Sarah, this police officer stops me and threatens to arrest me. Then
he tells me he gets a piece of all the action in town and that he wants
some of mine." The kid was actually shaking now. "The guy said that
no one would believe me if I said anything and that he'd put me in jail
and make sure I had a very unpleasant experience."

Les's jaw clenched. "What's his name?" His eyes blazed.

Peter took a step back. "I don't know," he answered shakily. "He
drove a police car, but didn't have a name badge. I have a place where
I drop the money, and he picks it up." He sighed. "Can I go now?"

Les hesitated.

"If we showed you a few pictures, could you pick him out?"
Dex asked.

When Peter nodded—although he looked like he wanted to
throw up—Dex turned to Les, who began thumbing through his
phone. Then he put up photos for the kid to see.

"Not him," he answered to the first picture. "And not him either. Wait, that guy there… that's him." Peter pointed.

Les's eyes filled with fire. It was obvious he was holding in an explosion; that was all there was to it. Dex felt the temperature in the room lower.

"You can go, but I want your contact information. I won't use it unless I need to, but this guy has got to be stopped." Les sounded every bit the cop he was, and it sent a zing of excitement through Dex.

"No way. I'm not telling you anything. You aren't the police, and I'm not going to get involved in whatever shit you got going on. I was only helping people—that's all I wanted to do. No way I'm going to jail over this because you got some axe to grind with him." He reached for the door.

"I don't want that either, but we need your help to try to get a bad cop off the streets. That's the only reason I'm asking." Dex loved that Les could let his heart come through sometimes. "I don't intend to get you in trouble."

"Okay." He reached into his wallet and handed Les his license. Les took a few notes and handed it back.

"Like I said, I won't involve you unless I have to. But your days of growing anything other than flowers are over." He glared, and Peter nodded.

"Yeah, I got it." He waited while Dex unlocked the door and then scooted outside and down the street like a scared rabbit.

Dex flipped the sign to Open once more and closed the door.

"What are you going to do?" Dex asked.

"I'll talk to Red. He needs to know what's going on. I won't break my word to Peter—even though that could put me in a difficult position—but the force has to know." He sighed, and Dex guided him to one of the chairs.

"But what about you and what he did?" Dex asked. "He allowed them to hurt you." He knew it in his heart, and that made him angry as hell. He paced the length of the store back and forth as he tried to think. "So help me, I'll…."

"Do nothing. Yeah, we know Williams is dirty, and that explains why he'd want to get rid of me. He knew I wouldn't stand for anything like that, and he didn't want me putting a damper on his other business dealings." Les's lips drew to a straight line.

"You think he did it on purpose?" Dex asked.

Les took a deep breath. "I think he took advantage of an opportunity, stepped back, and did nothing. I got hurt, so now I'm out on leave and he's able to do any damn thing he pleases, including, from what Peter said, getting a piece of the drug action in town. Jesus...." He clenched his hands, looking like he'd been hit with a brick. "The drug case I was working.... It's possible the fucker behind it was in the car with me the entire time I was working it. I should have spoken up and refused to have anything to do with him." Les lifted his gaze from the floor. "You know how it is when you have one of those moments? You know you're about to make the wrong decision, but you go ahead with it anyway because of pressure or because it's what you think your duty demands?" He huffed. "I should have just refused the partnership outright, but I had no concrete reason then."

"Okay. So what are we going to do?" Dex asked.

"Well, I'm—"

Dex shushed him. "Not I—we. What are we going to do? This isn't a 'you' thing; it's an 'us' thing. We're both involved, and we need to handle this together." He squeezed Les's hand. "I know your instinct is to go it alone, but you need to stop that right now. We work together. Okay?"

"But I don't want you to get hurt," Les said.

Dex glared at his boyfriend. "And I can say the same thing about you. When you care about someone, you stand behind them and support them. What happened to you was terrible, but you don't have to battle this asshole alone. Whatever happens, I'm here. If it means we have to come clean about everything and the store goes belly-up, I can live with that. I'll find another job and work things out." He squeezed Les's fingers. "But I'm not going to run like that asshole who left after you got hurt. And I'm not going to cover my ass. I'll take whatever lumps come my way. But one way or another, you are going to nail this asshole's balls to the wall. And then you can help get that drug-dealing asshole and the shit he's facilitating off the streets. Now call Red or any of the other guys you can trust and let's have ourselves a 'hang Williams's nuts on the line' party." Dex held Les's gaze and then snickered.

"What's gotten into you?"

"I just got this image of two tiny little bouncy balls hanging on a clothesline." He turned away because that would not leave his head.

Les laughed. "Dude, you're one sick man, you know that?"

"And you love me anyway," Dex retorted.

Les stilled, and Dex did the same. He hadn't meant to say that aloud, but Les touched his chin.

"I do," Les said softly.

"And I do too," Dex told him. He leaned in just as the bell above the door tinkled, then rolled his eyes. "You know, I spend hours alone in the store, and just about the time you say you love me and I want to kiss you, that's when I get a rush." He pushed himself to his feet, squeezing and then releasing Les's hand. "Go in the back if you want and make your phone calls."

"I'm going to sit here for a few minutes," Les whispered.

Dex nodded, then went out to help his customers.

DEX ALMOST wondered if he should simply convert the store to one that offered strictly children's and young adult books. Except for a few best sellers and recent releases, that was what he sold most of.

"What did you find out?" Dex asked Les when he had a few minutes of quiet time. He'd had quite a few customers and done some sales, but not a huge amount. Maybe selling only children's books wasn't the answer, but he had to do something to generate additional income and help bring people in. Still, that wasn't his most pressing need right now.

"Red said that he and Carter would be over as soon as the store closed. He asked if I wanted to make an official report, and I told him I wanted to speak to them first. I thought I'd let them make the call on how to go forward." Les bit his lower lip, and it was clear to Dex that Les wasn't completely comfortable with this approach.

"Good. Call Tyler and Anthony too," he offered. Les looked at him as though he was crazy. "This is going to dredge up a lot of things you probably wish you could just forget. You need to have your friends around you to support whatever it is that we're going to need to do. Like I said, you don't have to do this alone."

"Maybe. But I don't need some huge Broadway production number made out of it either."

Dex rolled his eyes. "Are you kidding? This is the perfect time for a great big production number, complete with a chorus line, cheerleaders, and beautiful boys in very tight pants. Go ahead and make the call." He stepped away when customers entered the store and let Les make up his own mind.

AT CLOSING, Dex opened the door for Red, who introduced his patrol partner, Carter. They were followed in by Tyler and Anthony, both of whom gave him a hug. Then Dex locked the door and turned out the lights at the front of the store, leading everyone back to where Les sat.

"What's going on?" Tyler asked Dex a little frantically. "He never asks anyone for help, not even when he got hurt. But he called and said he needed a favor, though he was pretty cagey about it." Tyler fluttered a little.

Anthony put an arm around his shoulder. "Calm down. I'm sure Les will tell us what he needs."

"But what if he's dying? Or he's sick? He doesn't deserve that." Tyler seemed about two seconds from calling in mourners and breaking out the black crepe.

"It's nothing like that, you drama queen," Les said with affection. "But it seems that Dex and I have stumbled onto something that's bigger than either of us thought, so I need to start at the beginning. Red and Carter, are you off duty?"

"Yes," Red answered, crossing his arms over his chest and flashing Les a skeptical look.

"Good. Just listen, then." He looked at the others. "Red already knows that I was watching Hummingbird Books, that I thought something was going on here. He thought I was imagining things. But it turns out I wasn't."

"I wish he was," Dex interjected. "Mom was selling marijuana to some of the old ladies in town who needed it for medical purposes but couldn't get it themselves." He looked at the police officers. "That has stopped, and anything I found has taken a one-way trip down the hole."

"But when the supplier came in today, Dex called me." Les motioned to Red and Carter, who were both scowling now. "I spoke to him, and I believe that he's out of business. He isn't your usual supplier."

"And you're sure of this how?"

"Because the kid nearly crapped himself when I spoke to him. He's a college kid who was earning a little extra on the side. I believe him, but I'll give you his name so you can check him out. Still, this is the least of our troubles. He told me that a police officer found out where he was growing the plants, and instead of busting him, he took a cut of the profits. Apparently this guy gets a piece of a lot of the local action." Dex looked from Les to the others, and Red's arms uncrossed and lowered slowly.

"And you think you know who this is?"

"Peter identified him," Dex said. "We showed him your picture first, then one of someone else before he identified Williams."

"Oh my God," Tyler gasped. "Your partner? Is that why you got hurt? Was he doing this shit then and you got in the middle of one of his deals?"

"You've been watching too much television again," Anthony said and then looked at Les. "Right?"

"I don't know. I doubt he was directly involved in my getting hurt, but he did nothing to prevent it. At least I don't think he did. There's no evidence either way," Les admitted. "As much as we want to get him for what he let happen to me, we may not be able to. But if he is involved in the drug trafficking ring in town, that would explain a lot about why I could never get very far with my investigation. And why he might have stood by and let me get hurt. It was a convenient way to get me off the case and just let it go cold."

"He needs a permanent change of wardrobe from blue to orange," Tyler said, rubbing his hands together in anticipation.

"Okay. No more Criminal Minds for you," Anthony told Tyler. "Your imagination is getting the better of you." Anthony tugged him closer. "Maybe we'll watch reruns of Queer as Folk and we can put it to much better use." Dex could see Tyler about to protest, and then he whispered something to Anthony, who shook his head. "We're here for Les, remember? Later."

The guys all chuckled. "What do you want us to do?" Red asked.

"Investigate Williams and nail him," Les said. "That's all I'm asking. I would prefer that you did it without using Dex or Peter, because I don't want to drag them into this. A lot of the customers that Dex is getting are families and children. Yes, his mother did something wrong, but Dex shouldn't have to pay for it. And he'd probably lose the business if this went public."

"But I will do whatever I need to in order to see that this asshole is punished for what he did." Dex sat on the arm of Les's chair, resting a hand on Les's shoulder. "This is more important than the store."

"If we get him, he may try to rat you out," Red offered.

"As far as I know, he's never been in. I doubt we're even on his radar. However, if that happens, then so be it. I want him out of commission. He's a dirty cop, and that means he's the worst kind of criminal." Dex wasn't going to back down, especially when he knew how this guy had hurt Les.

"We're going to have to explain this to the chief," Carter explained. "He's not going to be happy."

"No, he's not. But he'll be a hell of a lot angrier the longer this goes on. Besides, the main person he's going to be upset with is himself. You know the chief. He prides himself on a clean force, and finding this kind of dirt is going to piss him off big-time. He's also going to want it gone," Red explained.

Carter nodded. "And you're sure that there's nothing else in here?"

"I've been through everything and flushed it all. Containers have been thrown away. There have been people interested, but they have gone away disappointed, and I'm getting fewer and fewer inquiries." Dex lowered his gaze. "The thing is, I wanted to help them. They're elderly ladies who are in pain every day."

"I'm well aware of the medical marijuana failures here," Carter said. "It's hugely political. It's best that you don't get involved with it. While I understand the urge to help, it's still illegal and could cost you everything." Dex had never met Carter before, but he really liked the guy.

"We'll see what we can do," Red added. "I wish I could make some promises, but you know that's not possible. Make sure you're safe, and I'd suggest that you two stick together. If Williams gets wind of what's going on, who knows how he'll react? He stayed back while you got shot, so God knows what he's capable of. Especially when it seems he has a hell of a lot to lose."

"We can do that," Dex offered, leaning close to Les. "In fact, I like that idea. Making you breathless each and every night." He smiled as Les quivered slightly.

"Hey, that's not fair. No dirty talk unless you two are going to make out and we get to watch."

"Tyler," Anthony warned.

"Come on. They're hot. Not as hot as you, but still…." He smiled and leaned against Anthony, then looked at the two cops. "What do you want us to do?"

"Stay close to Les. Williams is a snake—he'll be at his most dangerous when he's cornered," Red said.

"I'm perfectly capable of taking care of myself and Dex. I was a police officer as well, and I didn't lose my skills just because I got hurt."

For what seemed like the hundredth time, Dex wondered what he had gotten himself into. Yes, he wanted justice for Les and for him to have some closure, but he didn't want him hurt. In fact, he was beginning to see just how deep the wounds had gone, and he wasn't talking about the physical ones. But the more he watched Les overcome them, the more he knew he was seeing the true man come shining through.

"I know," Dex said. "But it's more than that. This isn't just police work. It's about protecting the people you care about and helping to make it so that I don't lose the store." Dex looked around the space, and he could almost see his mother standing behind that counter, smiling, her hair pulled back into the bun she always wore. "This is what I have left of my mom, and I really want to keep it going. I'm going to need to find the money somehow, but I'll never get the chance if this isn't handled right." The thought of losing the store made his heart ache.

"We could simply back off, if that's what you want," Red said.

"No. This guy is hurting everyone. Get Williams out of his job and off the street. If I lose the store, then I'll deal with it."

"You don't have to do this for me," Les whispered. "You know that."

Dex met Les's gaze. "I do," he said quietly, loving the smile he received in return.

"I do too," Les told him just loudly enough to hear.

"What's all this?" Tyler said. He'd wandered into the front room and behind the counter. "You keeping the really good stuff under the glass on the checkout counter?"

"Quit being nosy," Les scolded.

"Yeah, sorry. Tyler is as curious as a cat and with about as much restraint. Come back over here, you…," Anthony said, holding out his arm.

Tyler shuffled back, carrying the light blue box.

"Those are my mother's tarot cards," Dex said. "I like to have them where I can see them during the day. It makes it seem as if she's here with me."

Anyone would think Tyler had won the lottery. "Oh! Can I take them out? I love doing tarot readings."

"Sure," Dex said, and Tyler lifted the glass and gently removing the cards.

He slowly paged through them. "Oh my God," he murmured. "Oh my God," he added a little louder, then started fanning himself. "Where did your mom get these?"

"At a local auction. She always loved them and recreated the missing cards herself." Tyler slipped away and returned to the checkout counter, where he slowly laid out each card. Then he pulled out his phone. "What are you doing?"

Tyler lifted his gaze. "Do you know what these are?"

"Well, I assumed they were Italian, by their design, but that was all I could figure out. Mom used them and loved them very much. She was always careful with them and said they were special."

Tyler swallowed. "Babycakes, these are more than special. Each card is a work of art." He turned his phone. "See that image? It's this card." He held it up. "They're not exactly the same, but very close, because each of these cards was hand-painted. I think they were made either in the fifteenth or sixteenth century. These are like the holy grail of tarot cards. Just one of these could sell for ten to twenty thousand dollars. Each card. To have a matched set of…" He counted. "…sixty-three cards! That's something collectors would kill for."

"Tyler's been collecting tarot cards for as long as I've known him. He has a number of special decks, as well as some pretty rare individual cards," Anthony said as he wandered over to Tyler. "He knows his stuff."

"Are you sure about this?" Dex asked, not letting himself really believe it.

"I'm pretty sure that these are really special. If you want to know more, I can send pictures of them to some friends of mine. One is an art specialist at an auction house. Marv is as old as the hills, but he loves tarot and has a collection of his own." Tyler took pictures of the set as well as some of the individual cards, both front and back. Then he gently packed away the cards and handed them to Dex. "I'd put these in the safe, if you have one."

Dex went in back and opened the safe, slid the cards inside, and locked it again. He tried not to think too much about his mom's cards and what they could mean for him. He wasn't going to get his hopes up. Besides, there were other, more pressing issues, like finding out what really happened to Les. Dex had a feeling Les was never going to be settled and at peace until he knew the facts. And the only way to get them was by catching this Williams guy.

"Red and I will talk to the chief and get his support. Then we're going to look into Williams's affairs. If he's dirty, there'll be a trail. All we have to do is follow the money." Carter grinned. "Luckily, I'm really good at that. You all watch out for each other and call right away if anything unusual happens. Don't try to take on this guy yourself, whatever you do." Then he and Red said goodbye to Les, turned, and headed for the door. "Les, we mean it."

"I know," Les sighed. "That's why I called you guys."

Dex let them out and locked the door behind them.

"Have you guys eaten?"

Tyler and Anthony shared a look. "We could eat," Tyler said.

"You can always eat. I don't know where you put it."

Tyler looked offended. "I'm a growing boy, and I have lot of energy and you know it. Most of the time, you're very grateful for that." He grinned, taking Anthony's hand, then turned back to Les. "Meet you at Molly's?"

"Great," Les said.

"We'll get a table. See you there."

Dex let them out, then he and Les finished closing up. When everything was done, he and Les headed over to meet their friends.

"DO YOU really think we should do this?" Les asked once Dex got him back to the apartment. "I mean, I trust my friends, but something like this can get quickly out of hand. We don't have any control over what Williams will do. He could take down the store if he decides to talk about it in court." Les sat on the edge of the bed.

"Then we'll deal with it. I don't know what the authorities can do. She's gone."

"Yeah. But federal law allows any property that's used in the commission of a drug crime to be confiscated. They could take the building and everything in it. Not that they would. I mean, you've helped law enforcement. I'll say that, and I know Red and Carter will as well. But…."

Dex sat next to him. "I know what the risks are. But I'm not going to let them back off for my sake. I can figure things out. You, on the other hand, need to know what happened. You deserve it, and if the police can get Williams to talk, they might also be able to clean up what's going on in town. Williams had his hand in everyone's pocket. So relax. Your friends are good cops, and they aren't going to throw us under the bus. I'm sure they'll be careful."

"I know they will." Les put his one leg on the bed, facing Dex. "Still, I'm worried about you."

Dex chuckled. "We're both worried about each other. I think that says a lot. Who can beat the two of us together? We already know that Williams has been shaking people down, that he's involved with the drug action in town, and we have a witness. I bet he's into other things too, and once we get him, more details are going to come crawling out of the woodwork." Dex lay back on the mattress. "Who would have thought that things could get so complicated, so quickly."

"Or that your mom was selling pot to old ladies," Les teased.

"You know, if I had ever used drugs when I was growing up, Mom would have beaten my ass black and blue. All I can say is that she must have felt very strongly about what she was doing in order to take the chances she did."

Les lay back next to him. "Do you really think that's why she did it?"

"I know so. You didn't really know her." Dex stared up at the ceiling. "When I was twelve, my mom came to school to pick me up. While she was waiting, she saw Kyle from down the street get pushed to the ground. My mom jumped out of that car so fast. I never knew she could move so quickly. She had the bully by the collar in two seconds and hauled him inside the school to the principal. Then she took Kyle home and read his mother the riot act when the woman acted like it was no big deal. Mom always stood up for what she thought was right." Dex sighed. "That's who she was, and I doubt that changed just because she got older." Dex swallowed and put his arm over his eyes. "I miss her."

"How long had it been since you were home?" Les asked.

"A couple of years. I was busy, and there wasn't extra money for airline tickets. The only way I was able to swing this trip was because Jane paid for it." He let his mind wander in the darkness. "I know I should have made more of an effort." He closed his eyes. "But I had no way of knowing that she was going to pass away so soon. I thought I had more time." He was determined not to cry, but it suddenly seemed like a pit of grief had opened up under him, and he had no idea how to avoid it. "And now she's gone and I won't be able to tell her the things I should have." He took a deep breath and released it shakily. He was suddenly on the verge of losing self-control.

"What did your mom think of you being in LA?" Les asked.

Dex wiped his eyes. "She was proud. Every time I got a role, she'd be sure to watch just so she could see me in the crowd scenes or as an extra. I swear there have to be DVDs or something in the house with the episodes on them. Mom wanted me to be happy, and

I thought being in LA chasing my dream was going to do that." He shrugged. "It didn't."

"What did it give you?" Les asked. "There had to be a reason why you stayed out there for so long." Les patted his arm lightly. "I can understand if you were having a good time, but that's not what it sounds like."

"It was an over-the-shoulder life. Everyone looks over their shoulder in case someone better comes along. I thought I had what it took, and I worked hard to try to bring it about. But it didn't happen, and instead of packing it in, I stayed out there until my mom had a stroke. If I'd given up years ago, like a sane person, I could have had some time here with her."

Les rolled onto his side. "Sometimes shit happens and all we can do is pick up the pieces. Your mom knew that, and so do you. It might have been nice to have had you here, but then you might have gotten on each other's nerves. She loved you, and she loved Jane. Do you think she was happy?"

Dex nodded. "I know she was. These last few years, every time I called, she seemed lighthearted, talking about the store and the things she and Jane had planned. They traveled some and seemed to entertain their friends a lot. It sounded like a good life."

"Then remember that. Your mom was happy. Yes, it would have been great if she'd had more time. I'd have liked the chance to know her better." He slipped his arm over Dex's chest. "You know it's okay to grieve and to feel loss. It's part of losing someone. There's no weakness in it."

Dex swallowed and didn't move. He knew Les was right. But Dex wished he could just get this hurt over with so he could move forward. Losing people was part of life, he knew that. He just wished he'd had the time to say all the things that kept going through his mind. He wanted to share what he'd found out about her tarot cards and what he was learning about the store. Dex would also have loved to be able to introduce her to Les as his boyfriend. But none of that was possible. So Dex lay on the bed and let Les comfort him, grateful he wasn't grieving alone.

Chapter 11

LES DIDN'T sleep well the next few nights, mainly because he knew Dex was awake, tossing and turning. He wished there was something he could do for him, but it seemed as if the loss of his mother had finally caught up with him. There was little Les could do other than listen when he told stories about her or just sit with him when Dex was quiet and thoughtful.

Dex opened the store each day, and Les spent a lot of his time reading in one of the chairs.

"You know you don't have to babysit me," Dex told him more than once.

Les gave a simple smile and then returned to his reading while Dex saw to the customers. One of the day cares in town had taken to coming in for story time, and that had resulted in the parents stopping by in the evenings.

"Anything happening?" Tyler asked from next to Les's chair, startling him out of his reading. He must have come in without him noticing.

"No. The last I heard from the guys, they were working on it, but the chief wants them to be careful." Les set the new Kim Fielding romance book on his lap. "It seems the chief has had suspicions of his own and is being very supportive. He wants to get Williams and everyone he's associated with."

"I guess it's good that it's quiet," Tyler said as he perused the nearest shelf.

"Let's hope it stays that way and everything works out just fine, with no drama."

"Pfft," Tyler said, patting his shoulder. "Please, I need some drama."

"Are things with you and Anthony cooling off?" Les asked quietly since there were customers in the store.

"God, no." He put his hand over his chest and turned his gaze skyward. "Lord save me from gay bed death." He crossed himself dramatically. Les expected him to start with the Hail Marys at any moment. "It's just that things have been dull at work, and with it being so hot, all we do is stay inside. That can have its rewards, but a little excitement outside the playroom would be welcome. Not a lot, just a little drama. No shootouts or anything, though."

"I'm glad you qualified that. Dex and I will see what we can do. Would you like it if we could hold off whatever is going to happen until you're available? I'll check with Dex and the two of us will try to arrange for it. Maybe put in an order with the gods of taking out dickheads." He rolled his eyes.

"That would be awesome," Tyler said happily. "I'm going to hold you to that." Then he wandered off to check out more of the books, and Les wondered where in the hell he had found such a nut. Then he thanked God for bringing Tyler into his life. Sometimes he was just the balm Les needed.

Les glanced up as someone passed by the shelves. "Thank you, and be sure to come again. If there's anything you need, we'll gladly order it for you," Dex said happily. The bell on the door tinkled as the customer left, and Les returned to his story.

ONE OF the things Les hated about law enforcement was the waiting. After a couple days in the store with very little to do, Les was beginning to go stir-crazy. He'd read half a dozen books and his foot felt much better, but his mind was about to explode. He was starting to understand Tyler's yearning for a little drama.

"Do you want to get dinner after closing?" Les asked Dex, who was leaning on the counter.

"Yeah, I'm starved. And then I want to go to bed. Every time that damned bell rings, I half expect trouble to march through the door." He sighed. "I hate this. I wish Red and Carter would just get this over with."

"These things take time. It's only been three days, and I know they're working hard. But they need to be careful." He fully understood how Dex felt. He was jumpy and anxious for answers too. "Why don't you finish up and we'll flip the sign a few minutes early. There's no one out front, and from the lightning show outside, there isn't likely to be anyone, especially once the sky opens up."

He stayed out of Dex's way while he took care of the day's proceeds and prepared his deposit. Then they left, locking the door and hurrying to the night deposit drop. They slipped the bag inside just as the sky opened up.

They hurried back to the store for shelter from the downpour. Dex unlocked the door, and Les followed him inside. They stood near the windows as the rain sheeted down the glass. "It looks like we'll have to wait this out."

Les put his arms around Dex's waist, holding him. "This won't last long," Les whispered.

"There's no rush." Dex sighed, his hand sliding along Les's. As he tightened his hold, rain pelted the pavement, thunder rumbled, and lightning split. But inside the bookstore, it was absolutely perfect.

"THAT WAS some storm," Dex said as they left the taproom, heading just down the street to Les's place. Cars hurried by, scattering the water still on the road. Leaves and small branches littered the sidewalk. During a break in traffic, they crossed the street. Once back inside, Les climbed the stairs with Dex right behind him.

"Are you looking at my butt?" Les asked, shaking it a little. He expected a chuckle but got a growl instead, then a pat as he reached the top.

Les unlocked the door, and they went inside. Dex locked the door behind them while Les turned on a light… illuminating a familiar figure holding a gun.

"What are you doing here?"

"Waiting for you," Williams said as though this wasn't a sudden life-and-death situation. "Did you think I wouldn't figure it out? I have eyes and ears… plenty of them. It didn't take long for word of what your friends were trying to do to reach me." He pointed the gun at two chairs near each other and then looked at Dex and grinned salaciously.

Les could barely control his rage as he looked at his former partner. With his short hair, crisp clothes, and warm eyes, he'd fooled a lot of people. Nobody had seen the venomous reptile behind William's clean-cut looks... until now.

"We know what you've been doing, and so do a lot of other people. And you know how these things work. Once someone talks, they all do." Les knew Williams was calculating, only doing what was best for him. "Instead of hanging around here, why aren't you talking all your ill-gotten gains and getting out of town?"

Williams laughed. "Who says I'm not already packed? I just have one little chore to take care of before I go." He smiled.

Les knew he had to keep Williams talking. The guy was getting itchy, he could feel it. "But why?" he asked.

Williams rolled his eyes. "Do you really think I'm going to stand here and tell you everything like I'm some stupid television character?"

He swallowed, and that was when it became obvious to Les that Williams was scared. He could see the fear in his eyes. All of his plans were about to come crashing down around him.

"You thought you'd get away with all of it, didn't you? The drugs, standing back and doing nothing when I was shot? You just let it happen, didn't you?" Les was getting angry, though he knew that was the worst thing he could do. For his sake and for Dex's, he had to keep his cool. "Why?" he asked again.

Williams leaned closer, pointing the gun directly at Dex's chest, though he spoke to Les. "Let's see... maybe because you're a fag and they're taking over the damned force. Half the guys in the station are gay. Then they stuck me with you. I couldn't ask for a reassignment or the chief would think I was homophobic and send me to one of those stupid sensitivity seminars or some bullshit. But I have a lot of things I need to keep an eye on. And you were this goody-two-shoes officer who wouldn't let go of the damn drug investigation, even when I made sure you got nowhere. I couldn't let you see the things I needed to do to keep people in line, so I had to get rid of you. The shooting was convenient." He actually shrugged. "But you figured that out."

Actually, he and Dex had, but Les kept that to himself. "You know you aren't going to get away with this. My friends know about you, and they'll check on us. We've taken precautions. If I don't call Red by ten…." That was just a few minutes away. "He's going to stop by. What are you going to do, kill the entire department?"

Williams leered, his beady eyes filling with even more menace. "Now that's the biggest bunch of bullshit I ever heard."

Les held his gaze, hard as it was to even look at him. The package might have appeared nice enough, but inside he was soulless and devoid of any redeeming qualities. "Okay. It's your funeral." Les smiled and leaned back in the chair, trying to seem unconcerned. He glanced at Dex, who did the same thing, even going as far as crossing his legs.

Williams's eyes filled with indecision. "Then text him… but I want to see the text." He clutched the gun.

The tension in the room ratcheted up as Les slowly got out his phone and composed the message. Then he showed it to Williams and sent it after he nodded. Normal 10 p.m. check-in. Dex and I are fine. Les hoped that would do the trick and that Red would understand what he was trying to say.

"What next?" Les asked. "Are you going to shoot us? Our neighbors are really going to be shocked when they hear gunshots." All he could think of to do was pile on the pressure. "You'd do better to get the hell out of here while you can." He stretched out his leg, glaring at Williams for being the reason his foot ached all the time.

"Not until I deal with the two of you," Williams said.

"How? The neighbors are going to hear anything that happens." He was really getting tired of this situation. Dex was scared. Les could sense the fear flowing off him, even if he was doing a stellar job of trying to hide it. Les had to get them out of this somehow. He needed an opening, but Williams was a cop, and he wasn't providing any. At least he hadn't tied them up, which meant that whatever he was planning, Williams didn't intend to stay around for very long. Time was ticking by quickly. He needed to figure out what the hell he was going to do.

"Les…," Dex said softly.

Les wanted to take Dex's hand to reassure him, but who knew how Williams would react? He needed something to defuse the situation. He could only hope that Red would understand what he had been trying to say in his message—the opposite of what it had looked like. They didn't have a regular ten-o'clock check-in. Hopefully the odd text would make Red suspicious. But Les couldn't count on it, not if he was going to protect Dex. And right now, that was the only thing on his mind.

Williams smiled. "I don't need to make any noise." He stood and approached Dex, who looked as though he wanted to rip Williams to pieces. Williams yanked him up by his shirt collar, hard enough that his shirt ripped right down the front, but Dex stood tall. Les could tell he was refusing to give Williams the satisfaction of seeing him cower.

Then he ripped the shirt in half, pulled a struggling Dex forward, and gagged him with the fabric. "See? Even if he screams, he isn't going to make much sound. Not with his mouth full." Williams pressed the gun to Dex's temple. "Now I can do whatever I want, and if you make a sound, I'll simply hurt him more." Williams pulled a small knife out of his pocket and pressed the button to extend the blade. "What to take first...? Maybe an eye or an ear? I'm not squeamish. After all, when you were shot, I watched, hoping you'd bleed out all over the pavement."

"You're a sick son of a bitch," Les said as Williams stepped back.

"I'll wait for now. I have some ropework to do first. I want to get you both tied up before I start carving my human turkey."

Les glanced around for a weapon of some kind. He knew he had a cane on the floor next to the chair but needed a chance to use it. Williams seemed to have come prepared and used his knife to cut off a length of rope he'd obviously brought with him. There was nothing Les could do as Williams tied up Dex. The gun was too close to Dex's head, and Les had no doubt Williams would shoot Dex just because he could.

While Williams was occupied tying Dex's legs, Les mimicked falling forward and hoped Dex understood what he wanted him to do. Roll to the floor, he mouthed, then contorted his lips into a grimace as Williams looked at him. "You bastard," Les growled more to give himself some sort of cover.

"And you're a weaselly, faggoty piece of shit. Like I care what you think. You dirty, butt-fucking excuse for a man." He grinned.

"Maybe before I'm done, I'll slice off your balls, just for fun." The man was obsessed and dangerous as fuck. Les started to wonder if Williams had been sampling some of the products the people he worked with peddled. It wouldn't surprise him.

"Les," Dex mumbled, his eyes overflowing with fear.

A firm knock sounded on the door. Williams stilled and it came again. He backed away, and Les nodded.

Dex closed his eyes, leaned forward, and rolled right out of the chair. When Williams whirled toward him, Les grabbed for his cane and swung it with all his strength as he came out of the chair.

He connected with Williams's head. A shot rang out, filling the room. Les's ears burned from the bang, but he swung again as the door burst open and Red and Carter raced inside.

Les braced for another shot, but it didn't happen. Carter had Williams on the floor, and Les got to Dex.

"Are you all right? He didn't shoot you, did he?" Les would beat the shit out of Williams if he'd done anything to hurt Dex. Les got the gag off his mouth and tore at the ropes that bound his hands and legs.

"I'm okay. I think his shot missed, but I don't know where it went." Dex got up off the floor, and Les guided him to a chair and looked him over closely. "Are you okay?"

"Yes. My foot hurts, but I wasn't going to let him hurt you." He smoothed Dex's damp hair away from his forehead and held him tight.

"I've called this in, and we have some backup coming," Red said rather quietly. "Are either of you hurt?" They both shook their heads as Les held his boyfriend. He needed to comfort Dex, who wasn't used to this kind of thing. And hugging Dex calmed Les as well.

"I'll get you two," Williams said from the floor.

"You shut up. You won't be able to do anything once we get through with you." Carter cuffed him, and Les guided Dex into the bedroom, where they sat on the edge of the bed with the door open.

"They're going to need to take care of him and get him down to the car and out of here. Once they do, they'll want to talk to us."

"That's fine." Dex hugged him tighter. "Do you think he'd really do what he was threatening?"

Les sighed. "I think he was just trying to scare us. Williams regularly abused any power he had over other people. He used to threaten things all the damned time." Though what he said was true, he purposely downplayed it for Dex. Les had a feeling that Williams would have done exactly what he'd said, but Dex didn't need to know that. It was going to be hard enough for both of them to sleep as it was. "Try not to think too much about it. He was out of his mind."

"Probably," Red told them. "Williams's cheese has definitely slipped off his cracker. Way off. The other officers are coming, and we'll get him out of here as soon as we can." Red stood in front of both of them. "You guys did a great job. Did you know we were out in the hall?"

"No, but I had to do something. Williams was getting worse by the minute."

"Then what you did was damned good."

Dex snuggled a little closer. "A hero."

"What?" Les asked.

"I said you were a hero." Dex smiled slightly. "See, you were wrong. You told me you didn't think you were up to being anyone's hero. But that isn't true. You're my hero." With that, Dex kissed him.

THE NEXT few hours gave Les a whole new perspective on what it was like to be on the other side of police procedure. Les gave the officers as much information as he had, concentrating on the fact that Williams had hated having him as a partner and that he had potentially stood back and allowed Les to be shot. He didn't talk about the store and what had been going on there. The more he thought about it, he doubted Williams even knew what was happening at the store. If he had, he'd probably have been shaking Sarah down. That was just the kind of guy he was.

"Are they done?" Dex asked barely above a whisper when Les returned to the bedroom after talking to the officers.

"Yes. They just need you to sign your statement. Both reports have already been written up."

Dex nodded and left the bedroom, then returned a few minutes later. "What am I going to do now?"

"Go on with your life… our life, I hope." They sat together on the side of the bed. "Why? Are you having second thoughts about the bookstore? About staying in town?" Not that Les would blame him if he was. Something like this was enough to make most people run for the hills—in Dex's case, the Hollywood Hills. And why not? If Tyler was right, Dex could sell those tarot cards and go wherever he wanted.

"No, I'm not. Julio sent my things for me, and they'll get here in a few days. I'm going to live above the store and figure out how to make a go of it. Besides, do you think one crazy police officer is going to scare me away? I lived in Hollywood. There are plenty of crazy people out there. They call them studio executives." He flashed a smile. "Like you said, it's over now, and we can go on with our lives." He turned to meet Les's gaze and then leaned against him. "That is, if you'll have a washed-up actor as a boyfriend."

Les drew Dex closer. "If you're willing to accept a gimpy ex-cop." They shared a smile and then a kiss.

The sound of a throat clearing pulled them apart. "We're done and will talk to you two in the morning. We called and had someone come fix the door." Red smiled.

Les's cheeks heated.

"Thank you," Dex said. Then Red left. The apartment door closed a few moments later. "Now, where were we?" Dex asked.

Les sighed as he closed his eyes, unable to give words to his feelings. The incident that had taken away his dream was behind him now, closed, and he looked forward to the future… to something and someone new. Without another thought about his past, he slid his eyes open to look into the intense eyes of his future.

Epilogue

THE STORE was decorated for Christmas, the windows filled with holiday books and glittering with cheer. Snow began falling as he stood out on the sidewalk making sure everything was perfect. Tonight was the grand reopening of the store. After discussions with Jane and taking some time to think it over, Dex had decided not to sell the tarot cards. Instead he'd contacted a New York auction house for an evaluation, which he was able to use to get a loan to update the store. It turned out that the deck was indeed from the early sixteenth century and given an auction estimate of six million dollars. That had provided more than enough collateral. Selling the cards would have seemed like letting go of part of his mom again, and Dex wasn't ready to do that.

"Everything is ready," Les said once he opened the front door. Les was just finishing his first term in law school and was loving it. He'd already decided he wanted to work as a public defender in order to help those unable to help themselves. In their spare time, they both advocated for a dispensary in the area to help people who needed it.

Dex looked around his newly renovated store. The sales floor had been enlarged to include the entire ground floor of the building. The back-room area was nearly completely eliminated because it wasn't needed, and unused space had been reconfigured. With the complete redesign, the store was larger, brighter, and more welcoming. He'd also been able to add a small counter for a coffee, juice, and smoothie bar, as well as a few baked goods that he got from Marcus at A Slice of Heaven. About the only things that remained of the old store were the main interior walls and his mother's Alice in Wonderland bathroom.

"I know. I just wanted to check everything one last time." He smiled and went back inside, shaking the snow from his hair.

"The store looks amazing," Les told him. "But I think I love the name most." Les had suggested that he update the name of the store to Sarah's. "We're supposed to open in five minutes. Social media has done its job, and the articles in the papers should help. Jane is behind the counter ready to take care of customers. So stop worrying. It's going to be fantastic!" He smiled, and Dex felt some of his anxiety slip away. It was just opening-night nerves, and he needed to deal with them, just like he'd help his young actors overcome them now that he was the director of the Carlisle Theater's Christmas Extravaganza.

"It's going to be good, isn't it?" He smiled, turned on all the lights, and flipped the sign to Open.

It was a momentous occasion, and the people in town didn't disappoint him. In the first hour, there was a steady stream of business—old customers, friends, and new customers all passing through the doors.

At seven Les commandeered the restroom to change his clothes, and Dex got the new reading area near the children's section set up for the kids. When the children gathered on the floor, there was barely enough room for Dex to take his place in front. "Tonight, our story is Officer Buckle and Gloria," he announced, holding up the book so everyone could see the cover.

Les emerged from the bathroom in one of his old uniforms— without the badge—and stood up front. "This is our own Officer Les. He's our friend, and he'll be reading the part of Officer Buckle." Les had tried to come up with a way he could make a difference in the community and figured the best way was to start with the children. They all clapped and laughed as Les twirled his cane like Charlie Chaplin before taking his seat. Then Dex started reading the story.

"I'D SAY we were a hit," Les said as Dex locked the door to the store.

"Are you kidding? We sold every copy of Officer Buckle. You're going to need to reorder children's books because the section is really anemic already," Jane added. "And these are the special orders." She handed him a stack of forms. "It's Christmas, and folks want to buy local."

"I'll get them placed tomorrow. And a backup shipment of children's books will be here Monday. I anticipated the sales." Dex was thrilled. This was better than he'd ever expected. "You all ready for something to eat?"

"I'm going home. You boys have fun." Jane patted Dex on the shoulder, and he hugged her.

"Thank you," he said softly.

"I'll see you in the morning." She backed away and Dex let her out, then relocked the door.

"I'm starved," Dex said. "You want to go out?"

Les shook his head. "While you were fussing today, I got things ready. Come on."

They left the store and used the back apartment entrance to take the stairs up. One of Dex's tenants had moved out just as Dex was starting renovations on the store, so he used that as a chance to enlarge and reconfigure their apartment. Les had done a lot of the work himself, with help from friends and using professionals when necessary. The apartment had been ready a month ago, and the two of them had moved in. It now had a deck out back, a larger living room, two bedrooms, an office, and a large kitchen. It was perfect for the two of them. Dex only had to go downstairs to go to work, and it wasn't far from downtown, where Les attended classes. The department had taken him back as a consultant. So it seemed they both had gotten what they hoped for, just maybe not the way they originally expected.

"Who would have ever guessed things would work out like this?" Dex said as he opened the refrigerator for something to drink.

"I know. It's like your mom is still here with us, looking after things." Les wound his arms around Dex's waist. "I know she didn't plan this."

"No. But I think she'd be happy with how things turned out." Dex turned around. "I know I am."

"Me too." Les tugged him closer, his eyes shining with happiness. For Dex, this was the ultimate dream.

ANDREW GREY is the author of more than one hundred works of Contemporary Gay Romantic fiction. After twenty-seven years in corporate America, he has now settled down in Central Pennsylvania with his husband, Dominic, and his laptop. An interesting ménage. Andrew grew up in western Michigan with a father who loved to tell stories and a mother who loved to read them. Since then he has lived throughout the country and traveled throughout the world. He is a recipient of the RWA Centennial Award, has a master's degree from the University of Wisconsin–Milwaukee, and now writes full-time. Andrew's hobbies include collecting antiques, gardening, and leaving his dirty dishes anywhere but in the sink (particularly when writing). He considers himself blessed with an accepting family, fantastic friends, and the world's most supportive and loving partner. Andrew currently lives in beautiful, historic Carlisle, Pennsylvania.

Email: andrewgrey@comcast.net
Website: www.andrewgreybooks.com

andrew grey

Catch

of a Lifetime

Some moments happen once in a lifetime, and you have to catch them and hold on tight.

Arty Reynolds chased his dream to Broadway, but after his father is injured, he must return to the small fishing community where he grew up, at least until his dad is back on his feet.

Jamie Wilson fled his family farm but failed to achieve real independence. Arty is hiring for a trip on the gulf, and it'll get Jamie one step closer to his goal.

Neither man plans to stay in Florida long-term, neither is looking for love, and they're both blown away by the passion that sparks between them. But on a fishing boat, there's little privacy to see where their feelings might lead. Passion builds like a storm until they reach land, where they also learn they share a common dream. The lives they both long for could line up perfectly, as long as they can weather the strain on their new romance when only one of them may get a chance at their dream.

www.dreamspinnerpress.com

Half a
Cowboy

Andrew Grey

Ever since his discharge from the military, injured veteran Ashton Covert has been running his family ranch—and running himself into the ground to prove he still can.

Ben Malton knows about running too. When he takes refuge in Ashton's barn after an accident in a Wyoming blizzard, he's thinking only of survival and escaping his abusive criminal ex, Dallas.

Ashton has never met a responsibility he wouldn't try to shoulder. When he finds Ben half-frozen, he takes it upon himself to help. But deadly trouble follows Ben wherever he goes. He needs to continue on, except it may already be too late.

Working together brings Ben and Ashton close, kindling fires not even the Wyoming winter can douse. Something about Ben makes Ashton feel whole again. But before they can ride into the sunset together, they need to put an end to Dallas's threats. Ben can make a stand, with Ashton's help—only it turns out the real danger could be much closer to home.

www.dreamspinnerpress.com

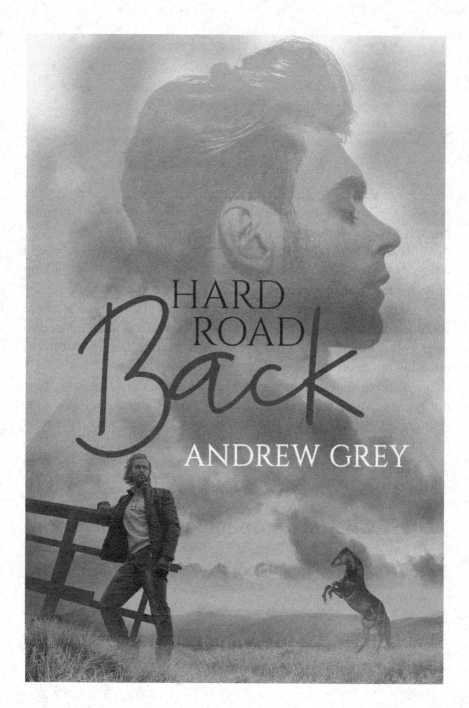

HARD
ROAD
Back

ANDREW GREY

Rancher Martin Jamuson has a deep understanding of horses. He just wishes his instincts extended to his best friend, Scarborough Croughton, and the changes in their feelings toward each other. Martin may be the only friend Scarborough has in their small town, but Scarborough is a man of secrets, an outsider who's made his own way and believes he can only rely on himself when the chips are down. Still, when he needs help with a horse, he naturally comes to Martin.

As they work together, Martin becomes more determined than ever to show Scarborough he's someone he can trust… maybe someone he can love. Even if it risks their friendship, both men know the possibility for more between them deserves to be explored. But when Scarborough's past reemerges, it threatens his home, horses, career, and even their lives. If they hope to survive the road before them, they'll have to walk it together… and maybe make the leap from cautious friends to lovers along the way.

www.dreamspinnerpress.com

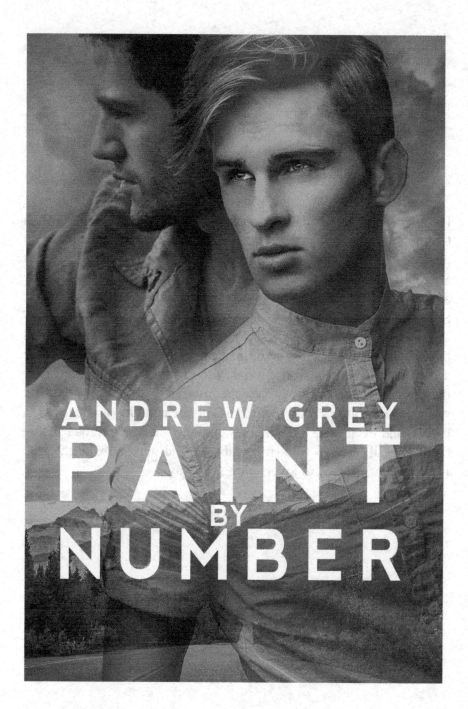

ANDREW GREY

PAINT
BY
NUMBER

Can the Northern Lights and a second-chance romance return inspiration to a struggling artist?

When New York painter Devon Starr gives up his vices, his muses depart along with them. Devon needs a change, but when his father's stroke brings him home to Alaska, the small town where he grew up isn't what he remembers.

Enrique Salazar remembers Devon well, and he makes it his personal mission to open Devon's eyes to the rugged beauty and possibilities all around them. The two men grow closer, and just as Devon begins to see what's always been there for him, they're called to stand against a mining company that threatens the very pristine nature that's helping them fall in love. The fight only strengthens their bond, but as the desire to pick up a paintbrush returns, Devon also feels the pull of the city.

A man trapped between two worlds, Devon can only follow where his heart leads him.

www.dreamspinnerpress.com

BAD
TO BE GOOD

ANDREW GREY

Bad to Be Good: Book One

Longboat Key, Florida, is about as far from the streets of Detroit as a group of gay former mobsters can get, but threats from within their own organization forced them into witness protection—and a new life.

Richard Marsden is making the best of his second chance, tending bar and learning who he is outside of organized crime… and flirting with the cute single dad, Daniel, who comes in every Wednesday. But much like Richard, Daniel hides dark secrets that could get him killed. When Daniel's past as a hacker catches up to him, Richard has the skills to help Daniel out, but not without raising some serious questions and risking his own new identity and the friends who went into hiding with him.

Solving problems like Daniel's is what Richard does best—and what he's trying to escape. But finding a way to keep Daniel and his son safe without sacrificing the person he's becoming will take some imagination, and the stakes have never been higher. This time it's not just lives on the line—it's his heart….

www.dreamspinnerpress.com

BAD
TO BE
WORTHY

ANDREW GREY

Sequel to *Bad to Be Good*
Bad to Be Good: Book Two

When a former mobster's past catches up with him, will it end the quiet life he's been struggling with, or transform it into something he couldn't have imagined?

Sometimes Gerome Meadows longs for the excitement of the life he left behind for Witness Protection. But when he stands up to a bully in a bar to protect a homeless man, his past comes very close to home—and it's no longer what he wants.

Tucker Wells has been living in a tent, surviving with the aid of his friend Cheryl and helping her watch over her son. When he winds up on the wrong side of an argument with some dangerous people, his already difficult life is thrown into turmoil. Gerome steps in to find them a temporary apartment, and Tucker is grateful and relieved.

Gerome never meant to open the door to trouble. His life and Tucker's depend on keeping his past a mystery. But as his desire to protect develops into something deeper, he and Tucker will have to evaluate what family means—and hope that their growing feelings pass unimaginable tests.

www.dreamspinnerpress.com